Vestige

E. H. Reinhard

Copyright © 2018
All Rights Reserved

AUTHOR'S NOTE

This book is a work of fiction by E. H. Reinhard. Names, characters, and incidents are products of the author's imagination or are used fictitiously. Any resemblance to actual events or persons, living or dead, is entirely coincidental. Locations used vary from real streets, locations, and public buildings to fictitious residences and businesses.

The scanning, uploading, and distribution of this book via the Internet or any other means without the permission of the publisher is illegal and punishable by law. Please purchase only authorized electronic editions and do not participate in or encourage electronic piracy of copyrighted materials. Your support of the author's rights is appreciated.

For more books by E.H. Reinhard, please visit:
http://ehreinhard.com/

CHAPTER 1

Clifford Walton III sat in a supermarket parking lot at the corner of Seventy-Ninth Street and Fifth Avenue. The area was brimming with prostitution. It wasn't a part of the city that he would have normally been in, but it was exactly where he needed to be at that moment. He'd been sitting low in the driver's seat, watching the intersection. A woman, blond with a lime-green skirt and tiny black shirt, had come and gone in several cars over the couple of hours that he'd been sitting there. The same car she left in always returned her to the corner where they'd picked her up. She wasn't a cop, and she'd been dropped back off just a minute or two prior.

Clifford turned the key in the ignition. The big motor under the SUV's hood rumbled to life. He crept forward and kicked on his headlights as he wove through the parking lot. Clifford exited onto Seventy-Ninth Street and made a left across traffic and a quick right at the corner of Fifth Avenue. The woman stood at the curb, ten feet from where he came to a stop. She immediately walked to his passenger side window, which he lowered.

"Hey, honey," the woman said. Her voice was soft and sounded young. "Are you lost?" She appeared in Clifford's window.

Clifford clicked on the interior light so he could get a look at her. Due to his truck's height, he could see her only from the chin up.

"Not anymore," Clifford said.

The girl had fair skin and looked as though she was in her early twenties. Her glazed-over eyes indicated she was high on something. Her makeup appeared carelessly applied. Her blond hair, obviously dyed, was thin and stringy. Yet beneath the sloppy presentation, she was rather attractive for a girl in her profession, Clifford thought, which probably led to her popularity on that corner.

"Did you need a ride somewhere?" Clifford asked.

"Maybe," she said.

"What do you mean maybe?" he asked.

"Are you a cop trying to run a sting on me? By law, you have to tell me if you are."

Clifford figured she might have been too new to her trade to have known better. Any seasoned hooker had to know that it was a complete myth that a police officer was required to tell someone that they were, in fact, a police officer.

"I'm not. Are you?" he asked.

With her mouth open, she chewed on a piece of gum, appearing to be in thought. She pulled the passenger door of his truck open and used the handle mounted to the windshield pillar to pull herself up and in. "Nope. I'm Kylie," she said. "What's your name?"

"Clifford."

"Like the dog," she said and slammed the door closed.

"I was named after the great men who came before me," he said.

"Um, okay," she said.

Clifford pulled away from the curb.

"This is a big ol' truck," she said. "What is it?"

"Defender 110," he said without elaborating further. She wouldn't care that it was one of five hundred or so. That it was the only one that ever came in black. That collectors would fall all over themselves to have it. That it had been meticulously restored from the ground up. That despite it being almost twenty-five years old, it would easily fetch in the neighborhood of two hundred thousand dollars. The truck had once belonged to Clifford's father. "Do you like it?" he asked.

"Yeah, it's cool. You're going to want to make a left up here and head back out to Seventy-Ninth." She pointed through the windshield at the approaching street. "We'll go to my place. It's just a mile or two away."

"I was thinking more along the lines of someplace quick and dark. I don't want to get out of my truck." He made the turn. "I know a place that would work."

She was silent for a moment. "I'm not supposed to do that," she said. "It's too easy to get busted."

"I'll give you an extra fifty bucks."

"I just can't," she said.

"How much?" he asked.

Kylie, the prostitute, adjusted her shirt. "It's not the

matter of how much. My manager is at my house. He deals with the money and makes sure I'm safe."

"Do you need to call him to clear it or something?"

She tapped on the small designer handbag that she held in her lap. "My phone is dead," she said.

"Look. We're going to do this my way or I'll find someone else. I can send your ass out of my truck with or without money, it makes no difference to me. There's plenty more selling down here."

She didn't respond.

"I'll tell you what, I'll give you an extra hundred dollars," Clifford said. "We'll go to my spot, get this done, and I'll drop you back off. Final offer."

She blew a bubble with her gum and popped it with a bite. "I want two hundred dollars," she said.

"Two hundred dollars?" He tried to balk at the price, as if he cared, or would actually be paying her.

"And whatever you're going to tip me," she said.

"That's your price?" he asked.

"Take it or leave it."

"Fine," Clifford said.

She turned toward him in the passenger seat. "Let me see the money."

Clifford dug his hand into his pocket and fished out his wallet. He spread it open and pulled out a wad of cash, which the hooker reached for. Clifford yanked it back. "No pay until we play."

"Drive," she said.

Clifford did his best to bury the smile on his face.

"Where's your spot?" she asked.

"There's a place at the end of a dead-end street a couple blocks away. It's industrial, no people around."

"Yeah, whatever." She reached into the small handbag on her lap and fished out a pack of cigarettes. "Can I smoke?"

"Wait until we get out. It will just be a minute," he said.

He made his way to the area, only a few blocks away. When Clifford had put his plan together, he figured it best to not take the prostitute too far from the area where he'd picked her up. Knowing where the high-traffic prostitution area of the city was, he searched maps online and looked for a good place to take the hooker once he had her. Clifford had found the perfect spot after just a few minutes of looking. A trucking company ran a school at the end of a dead-end street a few blocks from one of the most active prostitution areas. Clifford had scouted it out before driving to the supermarket. The giant complex, which included a trucking depot and huge parking lot against the train tracks, was fenced in. Semi trailers littered the lot. The sign on the sliding fence blocking the entrance said they were closed weekends, and it was. There wasn't a residence within a block. No one would hear her screams.

Clifford drove down the trucking school's street and turned around at the fenced entrance. He pulled up behind a box truck parked along the fence line on the right side of the street. The vehicle had been there earlier, and from the looks of it, some time before that. Clifford killed his headlights, clicked the gear selector into Park, and shut off the truck.

A wide center console separated the two front seats. Clifford reached for his door handle. "Hop out," he said. "We'll go in the back. There's some pillows and blankets back there."

He left the driver's side of his truck and met her at the back door of the SUV. Clifford pulled the handle and swung the big single door open. The back area of the Defender had bench seats running up both sides, and they had been flipped up. A couple of blankets and pillows were laid out in the big rectangle of the cargo area.

"Hop in," he said.

She obliged, and Clifford climbed in behind her. He swung the door closed.

"How do you want to do thi—"

She didn't get the words from her mouth before Clifford had lunged toward her and grasped her throat. He slammed her to the floor in back of the SUV and mounted her chest. With both hands, he held her in a vise-like grip. She swatted and flailed. The hooker kicked her feet and squirmed. Clifford kept his head back from her swiping hands. He was twice her size, and she wouldn't be getting him off the top of her. He slammed the back of her head into the floor as he gripped her throat with all his strength. After a minute and a couple of last jerks of her body, she was done.

Clifford released his hold on her throat. His forearms burned from the force. Adrenaline pumped through his veins. He was light-headed. He looked down at his hands, balled his fists, and slammed them both into the floor and to the sides of her head. Clifford let out a guttural scream into her dead face. She stared back at him, her eyes open and unmoving. He sat there, mounted on top of his kill, staring at her while he sucked in and let out huge breaths. She wasn't the first human whose life he'd taken, but she was his first kill in an unguided hunt, and she was the first he'd killed with his hands.

Clifford dismounted her and opened the back door of his truck. He grabbed the hooker by her wrist and dragged her body out. She flopped to the ground behind the big steel rear bumper of the SUV. Clifford leaned into the cargo area and produced a hatchet from a side compartment.

He turned his attention to the hooker's body on the ground.

"Time for my trophy," he said.

CHAPTER 2

I'd had the Monday marked on the calendar for weeks. I'd gotten my boat packed and hooked up to the Bronco the night before. My cooler was filled with ice and stuffed with waters, sodas, breakfast, and lunch. I was out the door of my house right around five a.m. After a quick stop at the gas station to fuel up my truck and boat, I was on the road and headed north on Highway 27. The drive to the bait shop near Lake Okeechobee took a few minutes over an hour. I'd been to the place before and knew that the later in the morning it got, the fewer my chances were that they'd still have shiners.

I pulled into the bait shop and parked off to the side. A couple of trucks with boats were already in the lot. Even after shooting the breeze with the old guy behind the counter and grabbing a free cup of coffee, I was in and out with three dozen wild shiners within fifteen minutes. The boat ramp I was headed for was in John Stretch Park—a small roadside patch of grass that had a couple of pavilions. The park had a free public boat ramp, but as with the bait shop, it was better to come early. The park filled up quickly later in the day, and I'd find myself waiting forever to launch. Thankfully, when I arrived I had to wait only a few minutes. I put the boat in, parked the truck, and motored away from the dock. The guy at the bait shop said the best fishing had been around the northern tip of Ritta Island, which was basically where I was launching.

Over the years, I'd been out on the lake more times than I could count. I rarely went solo, yet that day I couldn't find a single person who wanted to go. My father and mother, who both enjoyed fishing, were on vacation out west, visiting my aunt. I tried talking Amy into taking off work and joining me, but she had a sales meeting that she had to head up. Steve and the guys from the station were on duty. I couldn't even take Lucky—she had gotten into something and developed some kind of dog rash. The vet said it wasn't too big a deal and should clear up in a week or so. He gave us some cream to treat it but thought it best we keep that area dry. Taking the dog to the lake and keeping her dry wouldn't really work.

The boat ramp technically launched into the Caloosahatchee River, which I took west for a few thousand feet before it bent northwest. Off to my right, past a half mile of scattered trees and shallow water vegetation, was the island itself. I was taking the river up and around until it linked up with the lake. A few channels cut through the low-lying areas, but some of them were water-level dependent, and I wasn't familiar enough with them to know which were which. I made my right through the pass and into the south end of the lake. Ritta Island and a couple of boats were off to my right. I started in that direction but stayed far enough out that my opening the boat up wasn't going to be too much of a distraction to the guys already fishing. The northernmost tip of the island, which I'd been informed was the current hot spot, was a good mile away. As I neared, I hadn't seen any boats. That was either good or bad. I was going to have the best spot to myself, or the guys already out had tried it and moved on. After surveying the area, I got into position and anchored.

The northern end of the island was land as opposed to the scrappy bulrush, reeds, cattails, and a dozen other water plants that popped up from the shallow lake bed. The island in the early nineteen hundreds had a hotel and had been cleared for farming. A hurricane and flooding wiped the island clean in the nineteen twenties, and nothing was ever rebuilt on it. From the looks of it, passersby would never guess that it had ever been inhabited—not a stick of a human structure remained. Yet I remembered looking at aerial views of the area while trying to find spots to fish, and they still showed rectangular farming plots.

I looked left and right, but not another boat was in sight. I scratched at my shorter than normal hair. My girlfriend had talked me into letting her hairstylist try something new on my hair. What she'd done was essentially shave off everything on the sides then pile a bunch of goops and sprays into the top, which made it stand on end. The style didn't look terrible on me, yet it required way more time than I liked in order to avoid looking as if I'd just had a bowl cut. After a solid week of me complaining, Amy allowed me to go to my normal barber and have it shaved off.

VESTIGE

The sun had just broken the horizon to the east. The temperature was cool and the lake calm—a good morning for fishing. It had been a couple of months since I'd had the boat out on the water, and everything seemed to be operating as it should. I went for a rod and got it rigged up. I'd start out by casting a shiner on a float at the weed line. As I tied on a hook and float, I saw movement on the surface—there were fish, and they were active. I took a quick seat and reached for the live well. Before my hand could open the lid, I felt my phone ring. Figuring it was Amy just waking up and wanting to see if I'd made it here okay, I pulled my phone out. The call wasn't coming from Amy, though. The name on the screen was Dave. Getting a call from him that early more than likely meant he had a homicide that he needed the day shift guys to follow up on. I set my fishing rod down and clicked Talk.

"Hey, Dave," I answered.

"Did I wake you up?"

"Nope. I've been up for hours already. I'm on Okeechobee, fishing," I said.

"Fishing?"

"Yeah, it's my day off.".

"Damn. I forgot. Let me call in Steve."

"Well"—I looked down at my watch, and it wasn't even seven—"what's going on?"

"Dead female, appears to be a prostitute. Just a block or two off Biscayne in that part of town."

Biscayne was Biscayne Boulevard, and "that part of town" he was referring to was the area around NE Seventy-

Ninth Street. The entire area was ripe with prostitution, and no matter how many sting operations were run, the hookers and Johns always returned. Yet there had to be more to the story than that. A dead hooker in that part of town wasn't something that Dave and the night shift guys wouldn't be able to handle or at least pass off to us when we got in.

"What's special about it?"

"Strangled and missing a hand," Dave said. "Freshly chopped off and not on scene."

"Interesting," I said. "A trophy from the kill? A message? What?"

"Don't know. But she's still got her left hand, so it wasn't something to keep us from identifying her via prints."

"All right. Are you on scene?" I asked.

"I just got here a couple minutes ago."

"And anything?" I asked.

The sound of an approaching boat caught my ear. I looked over my right shoulder to see a sparkling red bass boat coasting up about a hundred feet off my right side. Two guys were on it. Both threw me a wave, which I returned.

"No witnesses, no cameras in the area, no nothing. I didn't see any kind of purse, handbag, phone, or anything around the deceased. I have a dead prostitute minus a hand. My next call was going to be to Vice to see if someone could come over and have a look at her before she gets taken off by Skip when he gets here."

"Crime lab?" I asked.

"They'll be here momentarily." I heard what sounded like Dave talking to someone else on his end of the call. "Let me give Steve a call and get back to it," he said. "Some guy just wandered up out of nowhere saying he saw a vehicle lurking around back here last night."

"Sure," I said.

"Good luck with your fishing. Tight lines," Dave said.

"Tell Steve to give me a call with an update later," I said.

"Will do."

I clicked off, dropped my phone back into my pocket, and opened the live well lid. I stared down at the thirty some dollars in shiners swimming around. I eyed a nice big one and began to reach. My phone rang again. "Son of a…" I reached into my pocket and pulled out my phone—Amy that time. I clicked Talk.

"Hey," I said.

"You made it okay?" she asked.

"Here on the water," I said.

"Good."

"I just got off the phone with Dave. They got one overnight. Looks like I would have been going in early if I wasn't sitting out here."

"So, you're not going in?" Amy asked.

"Hell no," I said. "It's my day off, and I'm an hour-plus away from the office out on the lake."

"All right," Amy said. "I just know how you are. You'll sit there and stew on it, then you'll start calling whoever is on the scene and pestering them, and then you'll get all up in a huff and go there, anyway."

I didn't respond.

"Which, if that's what you're going to do, you may as

well go now and skip all the screwing around."

The sound of splashing caught my ear. I glanced over at the neighboring boat and the guy reeling in what looked like a decent-sized largemouth.

"Nah." I shook my head as I said it. "I'm getting my fishing in. I didn't come all the way here for nothing, and I've been waiting to hit the lake for weeks."

"Okay. You go fish." Amy chuckled. "Give me a call back in a half hour when you're driving to work."

"Mmm-hmm," I said sarcastically.

"Love you, bye," she said.

"Love you too." I clicked off from the call.

CHAPTER 3

After calling Dave to get the address, I'd talked to Amy as I drove back toward the city. We hung up just as she was leaving the house to go to her meeting. As far as me staying out on the water, she was right. As much as I wanted to fish and enjoy my day off, it wasn't going to happen. I didn't have a line in the water for two minutes before the thoughts about that cut-off hand started to settle in. I cast a few more times and continued to dwell on it. I made a deal with myself that I'd leave after catching a fish. I spent another ten minutes on the water biteless before reeling in and packing up. I gave the bait I'd bought to the guys in the neighboring boat and headed out.

The stop at my house took only fifteen minutes. I unhooked the boat and quickly transferred all the gear into the garage. Inside the house, I took a quick shower and changed into a suit. I gave Lucky a pat on the head and was gone from my house for the scene off Biscayne Boulevard.

Patrol cars had blocked off the small dead-end street. I pulled up in my Bronco and allowed through and toward the scene. More marked cars, plus a few unmarked ones, lined the right shoulder of the road along the chain-link fence. On the left side was a huge parking lot behind another fence. Some trailers and box trucks were parked along the left side of the street. I pulled behind the last cruiser in line and killed the Bronco's motor, leaving the keys in the ignition. I wasn't guessing it would be going anywhere. I jumped down, swung the driver's door closed, and walked to the group of guys at the open gates of the trucking school at the end of the street. Steve stood next to Colt and a couple of uniformed officers. I didn't see Dave or anyone from the night team. I glanced at my watch—almost nine in the morning. Dave and the guys were probably back at the station or heading home.

Steve apparently noticed me and left the group to meet me as I walked up. "Morning," he said. "Couldn't deal with letting someone else handle it, eh?"

I shook my head. "You know how it is."

"Catch anything before you pulled the plug?" he asked.

"Nope," I said. "Skunked."

I glanced left and right, not seeing any body, though off to my left, I saw what I figured to be blood in the sandy grass along the road's edge.

"Is that our spot?" I asked and jerked my chin at the area.

"Yeah. Skip took her away about an hour ago," Steve said. "A woman by the name of Kylie Bowe. Twenty-three. A bunch of priors."

"How did we get her ID?" I asked.

"Tillerson from Vice popped over here right around when I got here. He knew who she was right away. Colt has some pictures of the scene." Steve waved Colt over. "You have your camera?" he asked.

"It's in my truck," Colt said.

"Grab it so Harrington can see the pics."

"You got it. Give me one second," Colt said. He walked to his truck.

Steve turned his attention to me.

"Who found the body?" I asked.

"One of the people who run the trucking school. A guy by the name of John Hartley. He saw her as he pulled up to open the gate and called it in right away."

"This was, what, around six this morning?"

"Right around there, yeah."

"Where is he now?" I asked.

"Interviewed, checked out, and inside the trucking building there," Steve said. "He said that he was going to shut down the classes for today but he'd be inside if we needed anything."

"Give me some more on this guy."

"Fifties. Clean record. Not too much to report on him. I didn't think there was any reason to doubt what he said was true. Again, he's inside if you wanted to talk to him."

I nodded. "Did you guys find anything else out here?" I asked.

"Nothing."

"Dave said that there was someone who claimed to see a vehicle over here last night?" I asked.

"Yeah. I talked to him when I got here. We have the statement from the guy, for whatever it's worth. He lives in that over there." Steve pointed at the side of the road that our cruisers were all parked on. Behind the chain-link fence was a giant oak tree sprouting up from a junk-covered lot. A small boat sat half sunken into the earth, and beside it was a rusty old van with broken windows. Random piles of wood and miscellaneous piles of who knew what were tarped over. Farther back in the lot was a bread truck on flat tires and what Steve was pointing at—an old Airstream trailer that was black from mold and dirt, not the sparkling aluminum color that it should have been. The trailer, like the boat, sat sunken into the ground.

"Someone lives in that thing?" I asked.

"Indeed. His address on his ID is actually on this street, so I'm guessing that he legally resides there."

"Okay. What did he say?" I asked.

"That he saw headlights turning around back here last night. He said he looked out and saw some big dark vehicle parked. About it."

"Time?" I asked.

"He couldn't say."

"No make or model or anything?"

Steve shook his head. "No make, no model, no plate number, and didn't see who was driving it. He also didn't see the woman get killed or left behind or anything. He came out of his little place over there when he heard all the voices from the police talking this morning. He kind of seemed like he was on a lifelong bender, so I'm not really sure how much weight his statement holds."

"All right. Maybe I'll go have a talk with him in a second

to see if he remembers anything else. Did Dave and his guys head out?"

"A little while ago, yeah. I told him I'd give him a call if anything broke."

"Okay. What about our guys?" I asked.

"I sent Garcia and Ryan to see if there are any girls out walking right now over by Biscayne and Seventy-Ninth. Tillerson said that was where she normally worked. Maybe they can find someone who knows our victim and knew who she was with or what exactly she was doing last night."

I nodded. "I suppose I would have already heard if the trucking place here had cameras."

"You probably would have. They don't, unfortunately. This isn't a depot or anything so no real need for cameras on the property. The John guy, inside, said that they run a classroom during the week and use the grounds for teaching drivers maneuverability skills. Then they go out and road test from there. They're closed on weekends, so no one was here last night when this happened."

I looked around. The trucking school took up everything to the north and east. The guy's garbage dump in the making—where onlookers would never assume anyone resided—took up the end of the street to the south. We stood a block away from the closest crossing street, which held a couple of apartment buildings. Perhaps some door knocking there could bear fruit.

Colt walked up with his camera hanging from his neck. He seemed to be working some controls on the back of it. Colt pulled it from over his head and held it out toward me.

"Just scroll to the right," he said.

I took the camera, looped the cord around my neck, and looked down at the screen on the back as I scrolled from one photo to the other. I let out a breath, wishing that I had been able to see the scene as it was found and not on a three-inch screen on the back of a camera. No amount of photos could take the place of looking at everything in person. Sometimes, the smallest details could bust an investigation wide open. Those small details could easily be overlooked in photographs. "Can I zoom in on this thing?" I asked.

"Yeah, here," Colt said. He came to my shoulder and showed me what to press.

I continued through the pictures. The woman, as I was told, appeared to be in her early twenties. She was thin with blond hair and dressed perfectly for her profession—a bright-green faux-leather miniskirt and a small black tank top. She wore black boots that touched her knees.

"The woman had some lacerations to the back of her head as well," Colt said. "I think her head was repeatedly struck against something while she was being strangled."

"The ground?" I asked.

"Not here if it was. The ground is sandy right here, and there was none in the wounds. Since this is a strangulation, and we have signs of a struggle, I took a fingernail scraping from her. We'll see what we can get from that once I get to it back at the lab."

The sound of Steve's phone ringing got his attention. "This is Garcia," he said, looking at the screen. "Let me take it." Steve answered the call and walked away from Colt and me.

"All right. So maybe dumped here, Colt?" I asked.

"Could have been," he said.

"What about a TOD?"

"I'm guessing around six to eight hours."

"Is there a way that we can tell if the hand was taken off here or not?" I asked.

"It was," Colt said. "The amount of blood, sand, and dirt in the wound, plus the way the ground was underneath the wrist would ma—"

I cut him off. "The way the ground was?" I asked.

"Yeah." Colt scrolled a couple of photos back on the camera and zoomed in. I could see some indentations in the dirt beneath where the hand should have been. "The ground here is all dug up from what I'd think is the blade of maybe a hatchet or something like that. We'll have to try to match up the wound and markings on bone with various weapons to be sure, but I'd say a weapon like that would be a safe bet and that the hand was removed right where she'd been left."

"Can we tell if she was alive or not when it was cut off?" I asked.

"Either dead or knocked unconscious," he said. "I'm leaning more toward dead simply because I don't see anything that says otherwise. If our girl was already on the ground when the appendage was removed—and we can tell from the dug-up dirt that she was—and if she was still alive, we'd have all kinds of disturbed ground from her kicking around and just generally trying to get away. There's none of that."

"Okay," I said. I swiped through a few more photos

before handing him the camera. "Any evidence or anything of interest on her body or clothing?"

"I'm actually hoping that I can lift prints from her skirt."

"Her skirt?" I asked.

"You saw it. It was that shiny plastic looking leather. Whatever they call that."

"Patent leather, I think," I said.

"Yeah, that. Skip is going to get it to me as soon as he gets her on a table."

Steve walked up while jamming his phone into his pocket. "So far nothing with the guys," he said. "They're going to hang out down there for a little bit, though."

"All right," I said. "Let's go try to have a talk with this guy over here again." I pointed my chin at the Airstream trailer mixed in with the garbage in the lot, and we walked over. Steve and I had passed through the waist-high chain-link fence and walked around a tarp-covered trailer holding what looked like an old refrigerator. We neared some cinder blocks lying in the grass, and they served as the step up to the Airstream's front door. "What's this guy's name?" I asked.

Steve pulled his notepad from his suit jacket pocket and stepped to the right to avoid a lawn mower buried in the grass. "Richard Meyer."

"Okay."

I stopped outside the guy's door and gave it a bang with the butt of my fist. I could hear what sounded like talk radio coming from inside. With a grunt, a man looking somewhere in his late fifties pushed open the door of the trailer. He stared at me, then I saw his line of sight move toward Steve standing beside me.

"Help you?" he asked.

Standing five feet away from the guy, I could smell a faint whiff of marijuana, alcohol, and a gamey odor that suggested it had been a bit since he'd bathed. Looking at him, I guessed that his last encounter with soap and water was somewhere in the range of months ago. The man had long gray-and-black stringy hair and a matching beard. His outfit consisted of torn-up and faded black sweatpants and a yellow T-shirt, also tattered, that I imagined had once been white. "Richard Meyer?" I asked.

"Yeah." He leaned against the doorway.

"Lieutenant Harrington, Miami Homicide," I said. "And you met Sergeant Walsh here earlier. He told me about what you said that you saw over here last night. I wanted to touch base with you on that."

"What?" the guy asked.

"I just wanted to go over what you saw one more time," I said.

"I don't think I saw anything that's going to help you guys."

"Just tell me what you told him," I said.

The guy let out a breath and scratched at his beard. "I saw a big dark truck or SUV parked behind the box truck over there."

"Hear anything?" I asked. "People talking or anything?"

He shook his head. "No."

"You said you saw it turn around?" I asked.

"No. I didn't say that I saw it do that. I saw headlights shine through my bedroom curtains. The only way that would happen is if someone was turning around."

"Okay. So, you saw headlights," I said. "Run through it start to finish for me, please."

"I was lying in bed watching television. A vehicle's headlights lit up my room, which faces the street. I rolled over and pulled the curtains back to look out. I saw a vehicle over there. I got up and took a piss and then went back to watching television. The end."

"Any idea on the vehicle's color?" I asked.

"Dark," he said. "Look, I did my good-citizen duty and came out to talk to the police earlier. This guy here already heard all of this. Why don't you ask him and leave my property?"

"Let's keep this where you help us out, and I keep pretending like I don't smell dope coming from inside your domicile," I said.

He didn't respond.

"Black, brown, gray, blue, green?" Steve asked.

"Probably one of those. Dark is all I could tell," he said.

I glanced at Steve, who crossed his arms over his wide chest. "And you couldn't tell if it was a truck or SUV?"

"Afraid not," he said. "Full size, either way."

"A large vehicle?" I asked.

"Yeah. Either a big SUV or a full-size truck with a cap."

"Do you have a time?" I asked.

"I don't know. I'd been drinking. It was late. Most of the channels had infomercials on, I think. Anything else?" he asked. "I've got some food in the oven."

I glanced toward the dead-end area of the street, behind the box truck and the location where our body had been found. I didn't have anything else for the guy at the moment.

"We'll be in touch if we need to follow up," I said. "Let me give you my card in case something pops into your mind that you may have forgotten."

I passed the guy a card and left his door. I heard him close it behind me as I walked over to the end of his trailer and stood below the window on the end, the one he claimed he'd looked out of.

Steve gave me a look that said he was wondering what I was doing. I held out a hand, pointing to my line of sight at the street. I'd noticed the positioning of his trailer from his front door, and my view of the street had only gotten worse at the window. The line of sight to where the woman was found was on too much of an angle. Whatever vehicle was parked there would have obscured the guy's view of anything happening behind it. The most he could have given us was the vehicle information, and it didn't seem that he had much for us other than the description of it being a big dark truck or SUV. I guessed it was something.

Steve and I zigzagged back through Richard's fledgling garbage dump and off his property.

"Don't think he actually saw anything?" Steve asked.

I shook my head. "He wouldn't have had a good line of sight."

"Now what?" Steve asked.

"I want to touch base with the guy who found the body. That and there are some apartments at the next crossing street. I want to maybe have Patrol do a little door knocking there."

"Sure. Let me go see if they can give us a hand with that, and then we'll head inside. This John guy said he'd be in the office. It's on the side of the building there."

"Sure," I said.

While Steve asked Patrol to do some door knocking, looking for anyone who'd happened to see anything the prior evening, I dialed Captain Halloway and let him know that I'd come in to work the investigation. He gave me a brief talking-to about days off then asked for an update—I didn't have much of one to give him. I told him I'd call him back when I knew more or would talk to him when we got back to the office. I put my phone away as Steve was walking toward me from a group of uniformed officers.

"We're set," Steve said. "A couple of the guys are headed over to the apartment complex now."

"Good," I said.

Steve motioned for me to follow him as he passed me and made his way through the open front gate of the trucking school.

CHAPTER 4

Clifford had come to the conclusion that, for man, only another man would challenge him as prey. He'd brought back trophies from hunts around the world. He'd killed lion, leopard, and elephants in Zimbabwe. Clifford had bagged a Cape kudu and zebra in South Africa. In Asia he claimed a record sambar and moon bear. Axis deer from Australia. He'd killed quite a few endangered species to spice things up. Clifford had spent twenty years traveling the globe and besting every predator and game animal on the planet. Yet it wasn't until he went on a trip to the Amazon and hunted the ultimate game that he felt truly challenged.

Clifford leaned against the mantel over the big white coral rock fireplace of his trophy room. In a ten-inch-by-ten-inch glass box sat a red velvet pillow. On the pillow's surface were the bones of a human hand. Clifford remembered how the hunt was presented to him. He'd been in Paraguay on a darting trip for jaguar. After a successful hunt, his guide, a man that Clifford had done business with in the past, spoke of something that his brother was doing a little farther north in South America. The guide claimed it was something new, something different. After expressing interest, Clifford learned that the guide's brother was running a darting tour similar to the one he'd just been on for jaguar, except that the trophy wasn't a big cat—it was a human.

Far from any prying eyes, in the middle of the jungle, the guide's brother was taking parties via helicopter to a hunting camp that had been set up a couple of miles downriver from a village of indigenous people. The first hunt went off without a hitch. Clifford had darted a male, posed for a photo, and the group went back to camp. The next hunt didn't go as smoothly. The villagers, armed with primitive weapons, were expecting the men. Three of Clifford's hunting party were killed. Clifford himself had narrowly made it out with his life. With an arrow sticking out of his leg, Clifford was lucky that the guide had dragged him back to camp. They were the only two who made it. Patched up but refusing an immediate flight to get medical attention, Clifford wanted to take one more trip to the village. That hunt featured live rounds. The hand in the box, and the scar on his leg, were Clifford's trophies from the trip.

He turned his back to the hand on the mantel and looked over the room. Mounts from his conquests filled the two-story walls. Some of the older ones were from his father, who'd turned him on to hunting at a young age. Clifford's home had been handed down to his father by his grandfather, then Clifford's father had handed it down to him. Between the three men, the home had been occupied by the Walton family for seventy-one straight years. The house was a four-thousand-square-foot relic built in 1926. It was the first home built in West Miami and had been registered as a historic landmark some thirty years prior.

As a child visiting his grandfather, Clifford had thought it resembled a prison due to its boxy shape and gray color. From the outside, the home appeared to be a smaller rectangle on top of a larger one. The larger lower level featured a pillar-and-arch wraparound porch, giving it an almost Mediterranean look. When it was originally built, the house was surrounded by nothing but acres and acres of nature and towering longleaf pines. The few roads around the home were hard-packed sand. By the time his grandfather had purchased the property, most of the surrounding land had already been sold off to developers.

The house now sat on the corner of a busy intersection and stood out like a sore thumb in the neighborhood around it. To the north was a city park, usually filled with screaming kids. A roundabout sat directly before the front gates to the east, ensuring a steady stream of traffic passing the property. While the home was still on a third of an acre, every inch outside the perimeter fence had been taken over by homes a quarter of the size of Clifford's. His father had spoken of watching the neighborhood form through the years.

A faint beeping filled Clifford's ears—the timer on the stove in the kitchen. Clifford walked across the white marble floor and left the trophy room. In the kitchen, he found his pot on the stove was bubbling and steaming. He killed the timer on the stove top and looked down into the pot. Clifford dunked in a wooden spoon and gave the water a swirl.

Most of the flesh had boiled off the hooker's hand, but

some stubborn bits of tendon remained. He leaned forward and set the timer for another fifteen minutes. By that evening, his mantel would hold the woman's hand. By that night, he'd be on the hunt, searching for his next kill. He had something planned. Something that would be his greatest challenge yet.

CHAPTER 5

We stayed at the scene until a couple of minutes after ten. I had John Hartley, the man who ran the trucking school, give me the details of how he'd found the woman. It was basically as Steve had said. John had pulled up to unlock and open the gates when he saw her lying on the ground. He went to her, saw the state she was in, and dialed 9-1-1. The fact that I didn't get to see the scene as originally found ate at me. We also came up empty with Patrol knocking on doors at the apartment complex. Either no one had seen anything or they simply didn't want to say that they did. There were more areas of town than not that had little interest in speaking with police.

I had just followed Steve into the parking lot of a small Cuban restaurant where we were meeting Garcia and Ryan for lunch. The plan was to grab a quick bite to eat then go over to the address we had on Kylie Bowe, our deceased one-handed prostitute. Her address was a house about a mile and a half southwest of where we'd found her body. While we had her identification, we had no idea who her next of kin was. Starting that search at her home was our first step.

The driver's door of my Bronco clanked and rattled as I swung it closed. Steve stood in front of a bench next to the mom-and-pop restaurant's front doors.

He gave me a smirk as I began to walk toward him. "You keep slamming the door on that thing like that and something is going to fall off."

"Don't listen to him, girl," I said. I paused and gave the Bronco a hard pat on the front fender, which caused a couple of flakes of rust to hit the ground.

"I saw that," Steve said.

"Yeah, whatever. Are the guys here yet?" I asked.

"They'll be here in a minute or two. I just talked to them. Ryan said that Garcia was getting something from Tillerson on the phone while we were talking. I told him to fill us in when they got here."

"All right," I said and pulled open the front door. Steve and I headed inside, and after waiting through a line of five or so people, I ordered a Cuban sandwich and a Coke from the woman at the counter. The business was more small deli than restaurant but had about as much business as it looked like they could handle. While we waited at the pick-up window for our food, Ryan and Garcia walked in and joined the line of people. A minute or two later, Steve and I picked up our food and sat at one of the few open tables near the windows facing NE Seventy-Ninth Street.

Ryan had put in his order and walked over to our table, where he had a seat. "We just got a lead on her manager," Ryan said, making air quotes as he said *manager*. "The guy goes by the name Coolie. Average height and build, African-

American. His real name is Leon Reese. Thirty-eight and a laundry list of priors. Current warrants to boot."

"Cool name," I said.

"The coolest," Ryan said.

"This came from Tillerson?" Steve asked.

"Yeah. He just called Garcia with it. He said he made a few calls and got in touch with a couple people. That was her pimp, apparently," Ryan said. He motioned to my sandwich, which I'd just taken a big bite of. "How is it? I've been here I don't know how many times. This place is a local landmark."

I chewed the mouthful of bread, ham, roasted pork, Swiss cheese, pickles, and mustard. Ryan was on to something. The sandwich was amazing. "Good," I said. "Real good." I washed down the bite in my mouth with some soda.

"Yeah. Nice pick," Steve said. "It's been a while since I had a Cuban that was done right."

"Good. Glad you like it. You need to try their coffee here. Unreal," he said. "Get one on the way out."

It wasn't the worst idea. With my early morning and chasing around, I hadn't quite filled my quota of caffeine for the morning.

Garcia joined us at the table. "Did Ryan tell you about Tillerson calling? With a lead on the woman's pimp?"

"Just did," I said. "Do we have an address for him?"

"His last known is no good," Garcia said. "But it's someone to look for on the streets down here. Someone will know him and where he's at."

"I'm sure plenty will," Ryan said. "It's just the little matter of if they want to tell us or not."

"No luck with pounding the pavement so far?" I asked.

Someone behind the counter called Ryan's number, and he got up to grab his food. Garcia remained in his seat and shook his head. "There aren't a lot of girls out in the mornings apparently. We rolled up on a couple of people but didn't get anywhere."

"And Vice told us that this was where she normally worked?" I asked.

"That was what Tillerson said." Garcia nodded. "What's next?"

"Steve and I are going to swing past her house. We'll break the news to anyone there and hopefully get something to work with, but after that it's back to working the streets, I guess. I'm thinking we won't hear anything from Skip or Colt until later this afternoon. All we have right now is her address, where she was working, and her pimp's name. Steve and I will check out her address. You guys keep going on where she was working and hunting down that pimp."

"Manager," he said.

"Right. Manager," I said. "We've started cases with a hell of a lot less. Let's just start checking things off the list."

"We got something as far as a vehicle," Steve said. "Big dark SUV or truck. While that can't be used for any kind of BOLO and won't get us too far in and of itself, tossing out that description to whoever we talk to down here might get us somewhere."

Ryan returned with a tray of food and retook his seat. "Where was her purse and phone?" he asked. "We didn't find either, right?"

"Not found," Steve said.

"What about keys, money, anything?" he asked.

"Nothing on her unless she had some cash or an ID stuffed in a bra or something that we didn't see," Steve said.

Someone at the counter called the number for Garcia's food, so he rose from his chair and walked to the pick-up window.

"So where are her personal belongings?" Ryan asked. He took a couple of bites of his sandwich, stuffing his round cheeks.

"Maybe left with the pimp. Maybe she didn't bring anything out with her while she was working. Maybe with the killer," I said.

"Do we know anything about her residence?" Garcia asked. "House, apartment, live alone?"

I shook my head. "Small house in little Haiti. A couple blocks from Little Haiti Park. I looked it up. We'll find out if anyone else is there when we get there, I guess. Getting a phone number on her should be high on our list of to-dos as well. We can at least try to get a location on it."

"And no registered vehicle, correct?" Ryan asked.

"We looked right away this morning after we got her ID. Nothing listed," Steve said.

Garcia set his tray down on the table, sat, and dug into his lunch. We rehashed the morning while we ate. After I grabbed a café con leche for the road, we parted ways with Garcia and Ryan, and Steve and I left for Kylie Bowe's address. Steve led the way.

We turned onto Sixty-Eighth Terrace. The neighborhood

was mostly small single-story homes that could have been built anytime from the forties until the seventies. Each house was set fifty feet off the street. I imagined that at some point, it was a neighborhood requirement that each home have a white metal fence along the sidewalk, because they all had one, though none of them matched. The shoulders of the two-lane neighborhood street were ten-foot-wide spans of sand and patchy grass that met the sidewalks. Steve, driving ahead of me, pulled into the sandy shoulder in front of a bright blue single-story house. I recognized it from the map photo that I'd seen when I looked up the address. Two cars were parked in the driveway single file in front of a single-car garage door. Inside a screen door, the front door was open—it appeared as if someone was there. I pulled in behind Steve and stepped out of the Bronco.

"This is us here," Steve said, nodding at the house as he closed the door on his unmarked cruiser. The home couldn't have been much over a thousand feet. The roof looked as though it was in need of help. White shutters were bolted to the blue exterior. The yard was entirely white gravel.

I nodded and opened the white fence gate that blocked the sidewalk leading to the front door. After following me in, Steve clicked it closed. I walked to the front door and saw a man in a red T-shirt and shorts appear in the doorway.

"Afternoon," I said as I approached.

The guy froze for a moment before cussing, spinning around, and bolting into the home. "Runner," I shouted to Steve. I broke into a run for the side of the house and shot out into the backyard. I caught the color red streaking across the gravel toward a six-foot-high wooden fence at the back of the property. He had only twenty feet on me. The guy leapt, trying to catch the top of the fence and kick himself over. The old weathered wood wasn't going to hold his weight. The second he grabbed on, the top of the fence boards broke away and sent him falling flat on his back to the gravel on our side of the fence. I was on him before he could catch his breath. I secured a wrist and rolled him as I mounted his back.

"In the back!" I shouted to Steve.

I took the guy's other wrist and yanked my cuffs from my hip. The sound of Steve crunching through the gravel came a second later. He came to my side to assist, and I linked the guy up.

CHAPTER 6

"What the hell were you running for?" I asked. Steve and I lifted the guy to his feet. He tensed up and yanked against our grip.

"That's not going to end well," Steve said. "Who else is in the house?"

"No one," he said.

I jerked my chin at the house, indicating for Steve to check. "I'm taking him to your car," I said.

Steve confirmed, and I walked the guy around the house, out through the fence to the street, and sat him in the back of Steve's cruiser. I stood in the open doorway of the car. "Do you want to tell me what that was just about?" I asked.

"Man, this is some bullshit," the guy said.

"What is?" I asked.

"Who told y'all where I was?" he asked.

"We don't even know who you are." I looked the guy over. He had short black hair, and tattoos littered his neck and arms. He wore some big gaudy gold watch filled with what I was certain weren't diamonds. He wore red from head to toe—shirt red, shorts red, shoes red. I put him around his late thirties. I had a good idea I knew who I was looking at and why he ran.

"So, do you want to tell me your name and talk a bit, or are we just going to head straight to the station?"

Before he said a word, a noise caught my ear. It sounded like Steve shouting at someone. I heard it again, and it was definitely Steve barking orders. I swung the car door of the cruiser closed and jogged to the front door of the house as I drew my service weapon. Upon entering, I saw Steve linking up a dark-haired woman on the living room floor. A rifle, which looked like some form of an AR, sat a few feet away on the tile between the living room and kitchen.

"What the hell is going on?" I asked.

"Make sure no one else is in here," Steve said.

I went to the kitchen then down the short hallway to the pair of bedrooms and single bathroom. The home was a mess. Garbage and clutter filled every corner. The bedrooms' furnishings didn't consist of much more than mattresses on dingy carpet. I spotted a few more firearms and quite a bit of cash in the larger of the two bedrooms. I returned to the living room and holstered my weapon. "We're clear," I said.

Steve took the woman from the living room tile to the couch, where he sat her down. He turned and looked at me. "I went to the back door to knock. Just like the front, the inner door was open. Through the screen door, I see this one here"—Steve pointed at the woman—"dragging a rifle by the barrel across the kitchen. I instruct her to drop it, which she did, then I entered and secured her."

"I was just moving it," she said. "Trying to get it so it

wasn't in the open. Coolie always said if the cops show, make sure all the guns are out of view. He's a felon. I wasn't trying to do anything, I swear."

The woman sniffled. Her face looked skeletal, as if she needed to gain a solid fifteen or twenty pounds. My best guess was that her appearance was due to drug use. She wore a loose-fitting white T-shirt and gray leggings. I figured her for somewhere in her thirties.

"What's your name?" I asked.

"Michelle Dirol," she said. Her eyes left me and glanced quickly at a small zippered bag, about the size of a woman's wallet, on the glass coffee table. As fast as her eyes left me, they returned. A blink and I would have missed it.

"What's in the kit?" I asked.

"What?"

"The kit on the table you just looked at. Heroin?"

"That's not mine," she said.

"Right," I said. "The firearms, cash in the back, and the drugs are going to make a hat trick of charges for someone."

"None of it's mine," she said.

"Do you live here?" I asked.

She nodded.

"Your house or someone else's?" I asked.

"I rent it."

"But under your name?"

She nodded.

"Then it's all yours unless someone else claims it."

"It's not mine. I swear!"

"Who all lives here?" I asked.

"Coolie, me, Ashley, and Kylie. Sometimes other people come and go."

"Coolie is Leon Reese? The guy in the red who just ran from here?" I asked.

She nodded.

"Where is everyone else?" I asked.

"Ashley is in Orlando. I don't know where Kylie is."

"Kylie is why we're here," I said.

"Well, I haven't seen her."

"She's dead," I said.

She balked as if I was lying to her. "No, she's not. I just saw her last night."

"Sorry," I said. "But she was found this morning."

The woman on the couch furrowed her brow but didn't shed any tears for her dead housemate. She didn't ask how Kylie had died or why or anything. She just sat there.

"Were you close?" Steve asked.

The woman sniffed. "We weren't," she said. "Not really."

"But you lived together?" I asked.

"Not by choice," she said.

"What do you mean?" I asked.

"Coolie moved her in here about six months ago without even asking me."

"Someone who isn't on your lease moved someone into your place? Ever think of maybe saying she couldn't live here?"

"It's complicated," she said.

"Sounds like it," I said. "Did you and she get along?"

"Not really," she said.

"So, you didn't like her and didn't like that she lived here. That sounds like motive," Steve said.

She rolled her eyes at Steve. "I didn't do shit. And I was here all night."

"Anyone who can corroborate that?" I asked.

"Coolie. Probably some other people if they really need to."

"Coolie is what to you?" Steve asked.

"He's my boyfriend," she said.

"Was he Kylie's boyfriend as well?" Steve asked. "Or just manager?"

She didn't respond.

"What is Kylie's phone number?" I asked.

"It's in my phone," she said. "On the counter in the kitchen."

Steve fetched the phone. The woman, Michelle, gave him the instructions on how to get into her contact list and get the number. Steve sent off a text with the phone number to Wade from our tech unit and asked him to have the number tracked.

"You said you last saw her yesterday. What time?" I asked.

"Last night. Technically, I guess it was this morning. Maybe around two or so. She brought some guy ba…" Her sentence trailed off. "Two o'clock in the morning."

"And that was here at the house that you saw her. But then nothing after that?" I asked.

She nodded.

"Where was she working last night?"

She didn't respond.

"Look, we're not stupid. We know what she was doing. We know what was going on here. We don't care about any of that right now. We're just trying to find out who killed her, and we need to try to put together a timeline of her night."

"You'll want to go ask Coolie," she said. "He was with her most of the night like his ass always is. Or was, I should say."

"I'll be back," I said.

I left Steve with the woman and walked outside. Mr. Reese was staring at me through the car window as I walked up. I pulled open the door. "Mr. Reese."

"Yeah," he said.

"What were you running for now?"

"Exercise," he said. "Come on, you know why I was running. I have warrants."

"We didn't come here for you," I said.

"Then unhook me and let me the hell out of here," he said.

I gave him a look, which was all that was needed to tell him that wasn't going to happen. "Tell me about Kylie," I said.

"What about her?"

"What's your relationship with her?" I asked.

"I don't have a relationship with her. She just lives in the same house, you know?"

"No, I don't," I said. "But speaking of the house. We got a lot of cash in that back room. Some guns and drugs too.

That doesn't look good with your history."

"None of it's mine," he said.

"That's so weird. The woman inside said the same thing. But, with you being a felon, that doesn't matter."

"Did you have a search warrant to go in there?" he asked.

"My partner saw the woman inside with a firearm. With you running and a person armed inside, he believed it necessary to detain her until we had the situation under control."

The guy let out a puff of air and slumped back in his seat. "What are you, Vice?"

I shook my head. "Homicide. Kylie Bowe was murdered early this morning."

"What?" he asked. "Nah. No way. What are you trying to do by saying that?"

"It's the truth. That's why we're here. We're looking to make contact with family of hers. Or people who know where she was or what she was doing last night."

"Man, shit," he said. He shook his head and looked down.

"When was the last time you saw her?" I asked.

"Last night," he said.

"Last night when?"

"Two something in the morning," he said.

"Where?"

"Around Biscayne," he said.

"Crossing street?" I asked.

"Seventy-Ninth. Straight across from the big supermarket."

It was right where we'd heard she worked. The mention of the supermarket across the street registered on my radar.

There was a chance we could get her on some outdoor parking lot video—if they had any.

"She works the corner there?" I asked.

He barely nodded.

"Where exactly?" I asked.

"There's a bus stop there on the corner with a big empty lot behind it. East of the park is an old shopping center that's out of business. She goes up and down there."

"Where were you that you saw her there?"

"There's some apartments back behind that empty lot. I park there and watch her. I provide security or whatever you want to call it for a couple of girls. I bounce around and just kind of make sure that everything is okay with them."

"Do you hold their money too?" I asked. "Take your cut?"

"All I do is provide security. Nothing more."

"Sure," I said. "What was the last vehicle she left in?"

"Shit," he mumbled again.

"What?" I asked.

"I wasn't there. I was a couple miles away checking in on someone else."

"That security you provide is a little lacking, don't you think?" I asked.

He didn't respond.

"Was there anyone else working with her in that spot last night?" I asked.

"I guess you could say that there are a couple of girls who are regulars right there."

"Names for any of them?" I asked.

"I don't work security for them, so them and their names ain't my concern."

"Right," I said. "So, you saw Kylie around two and then not again? She lives here, the same place as you, and never returned, and you didn't think that was odd?"

"Hell yeah, I thought it was odd."

"Try calling her?"

"A couple of times," he said. "I thought maybe she just stayed with someone for the night."

"Is that something that frequently happens?" I asked.

"I wouldn't say frequently, but it has. She normally calls me if that sort of thing is going on, though."

"But no call?" I asked.

He shook his head.

"Harrington," I heard.

I glanced back to see Steve in the home's front doorway.

"Hang tight for me, Mr. Reese." I closed the car door and walked toward the house.

Steve remained in the doorway, checking over his shoulder, probably to make sure the woman was staying put. He kept his voice low so she wouldn't be able to overhear. "We're going to have to get Patrol or someone out here for the drugs, guns, and cash," Steve said.

"I agree. Anything on getting a GPS location?" I asked.

Steve shook his head. "I just got a text from Wade a minute ago. No signal. Apparently, she had a sister, though. First name is Selma. Ms. Dirol says she's a local."

"Same last name?" I asked.

"She didn't know but says she isn't married."

"Okay. We'll have to see what if anything we can find on her."

"Anything from our jogger?" Steve asked.

"Just the exact area that Kylie Bowe worked. I'm going to send off a text to Garcia and see if he and Ryan can get with the businesses there about any outdoor video. There's a shopping center and supermarket across the street. Maybe they caught something."

"All right. Nothing else with our pimp, though? He wasn't with her last night?"

"He says not at the time in question. But who knows? He says he was somewhere else," I said.

"Do you think that we should maybe dig into him?" Steve asked. "Or the Dirol woman. She flat out gave us her motive."

"Run her and see what we get," I said as I fired off a text to Garcia.

CHAPTER 7

Clifford leaned back in his chair and stared across the room at the pig head mounted to the wall—his first kill. Well, not technically, but his father wasn't going to let him mount the family dog's head to the wall. After catching Clifford with Scooter, the beagle, his father gave him a long talk about the meaning of life. Clifford had given his father some kind of naive innocent-kid response about seeing his father kill animals and not knowing any better. With that, his father got him into hunting—so Clifford could learn the value of life and what was truly involved in taking one. At least that was what the story had turned into over the years.

The truth was, Clifford had smashed the family dog's head in with a hammer, and his father beat him within an inch of his life for doing it. After the beating, he was pulled out of school and locked in his room for weeks while he healed. The hunting began as an extension of his punishment. His father thought he could scare him out of killing by making him field dress a pig that he shot. Clifford was fine with dressing the pig, and it only added to his desires. He learned that he enjoyed the thrill of the hunt and found the blood and internal organs interesting. His father told him later in life that it was that very day that he knew something wasn't quite right with Clifford, so he kept taking him hunting as a way to get him to not begin doing "other things." His father never did expound on what those "other things" were, but Clifford was pretty certain that he was referring to murder. Thinking back, Clifford questioned why it took him until his mid-forties before he ever took a human life.

Clifford took his eyes from the pig and brought the jewelers glasses back down from their resting spot on the mostly bald top of his head. He stared through the magnifying lenses and drilled a tiny hole in the spot that he'd marked. He repeated the process again and again. When finished, he set the glasses down on the edge of the table where he worked. Clifford wiped the sweat from his forehead on his sleeve. The hand bones had been boiled clean, and each finger bone received a hole for fishing line. The jagged and splintered wrist bones had been discarded.

Before Clifford on the table was a pile of twenty-seven bones. He began to set them where he thought they were supposed to go, arranging them by size and how he believed they should look. If one or two were out of place, he didn't care.

He unspooled the clear twenty-five-pound test fluorocarbon fishing line and snipped off a section. He'd used the technique of drilling holes and using the line on the hand he'd picked up in the Amazon. It had worked well enough for him that he didn't stray too far from using the method.

Clifford tied a knot in the line and began slipping the other end through the bone he'd selected for her index finger. One bone after the other, he tied them until the hand was complete. Clifford walked the hand over to the mantel and its waiting glass case. He set the hand on the velvet pillow and closed the glass lid. Clifford gave it a look, wondering if they'd found the woman's body the hand had once belonged to. He'd left her body right where he killed her. He'd tossed her phone and purse from his SUV on the drive home.

Clifford left the trophy room and made a right at the hallway stemming off the living room. He walked to one of the home's spare bedrooms that had been converted to a home office. Clifford entered, rolled back his desk chair, and had a seat. He wiggled his computer mouse. As he waited for his computer to boot up, he went through his mental checklist for the night. He nodded as he thought. Purchasing the body armor had been a wise decision for what he was planning to do.

CHAPTER 8

I glanced at my watch. We were inching up on one in the afternoon. A cussing and flailing Ms. Dirol had just been taken from the home and placed in the back of a cruiser by a pair of uniformed officers. Upon running her name, we learned she was also a convicted felon and had a couple of outstanding warrants like her boyfriend, Leon Reese.

One of the uniformed officers approached Steve and me at Steve's car. I recognized the guy as one of those on the scene where Kylie Bowe's body was found.

"Do you want us to go through this place?" he asked.

I nodded. "Guns, cash, and drugs. Get it all logged and out of here."

"You got it. Was there anything that you were specifically looking for inside?"

"We didn't come here looking for anything. We came here to hopefully find next of kin on the deceased from this morning."

"The woman missing the hand?" he asked.

"Correct. This was the address where she resided. The guy in your car was her pimp. The other woman, a roommate of the deceased. We're not sure they had anything to do with what happened to her, but if you find a missing hand in the freezer or something, give us a jingle."

"Okay. We'll keep our eyes open and get everything else collected and logged. If you need the report or to see anything, just contact the Northside District."

"Appreciate it," I said.

The officer walked to the house.

"Do we need anything else out here?" Steve asked.

"No. These two are going to be in lockup if we need them," I said. "Let's see what we can get on this sister."

Steve went to the driver's door of his car and hopped in. I stood outside his open door as he used his car's computer to search for the name of a woman with the same surname as Kylie. The computer showed results almost immediately.

"She's only twenty," Steve said. "The address is in Aventura."

Aventura was one of the nicer areas of greater Miami, about twenty-five minutes north of us. I imagined the home where Bowe's sister lived would be out of reach for someone two years out of high school. Most of the places in that part of town were upward of half a million dollars. "Lives with her parents, maybe," I said. "Or alone with wealthy parents footing the bill. Pull up the address and see what you find."

Steve punched away at the computer. "We have a Patrick Bowe at that address, age forty-five." He clicked away at the keyboard. "And a Megan Bowe, forty-three."

"The right age for parents," I said.

"That they are. Do you want to take a drive up there and see what we get?" Steve asked.

"Yeah. On the drive, I'm going to give the guys a call to check in. Call the captain and let him know we're headed up that way."

"Sure," Steve said. "Did he give you any shit about coming in today?".

"A little," I said. "Nothing too serious." I started to my truck and spoke over my shoulder. "I'll follow you."

I jumped in my truck, slammed the door, and turned the key in the ignition. The starter made a single click. "Dammit," I said. I gave it a second, asked her to start, then tried the ignition again. The starter cranked, and the motor fired. "Thank you," I said. It had been the third or fourth time in a month that the truck's starter had given me some grief. A new starter for the Bronco was sitting in a box in my garage, and it looked as though I'd be swapping it out over the weekend. We started east and then north on Biscayne, which would take us the entire way to Aventura. I dialed Garcia ten minutes into the drive. He picked up in a couple of rings.

"Anything at the house?" he answered.

Over the exhaust noise and droning of the Bronco's tires, I gave him the highlights of what went down. He said that he and Ryan had checked the supermarket and found that while they did have outdoor cameras, none faced the street. The supermarket's front entrance faced east, and so did the cameras. We needed something that faced south. Garcia had said that they also went through the other businesses in the shopping center but came up empty. I told him to continue trying to talk to anyone they could find and said I'd be in touch after we made our stop at the Aventura address.

Steve, driving ahead of me, flicked on his right directional and turned off Biscayne onto NE 207th Street. A quarter mile up, he got into the left turn lane and, when a gap in the traffic presented itself, made the turn into the Aventura Lakes subdivision. A pavered bridge took us toward a guard shack. To our left and right, beyond the water and fountains, were the homes of the neighborhood.

Steve stopped at the guard shack, and a man walked from the building to his window. The two appeared to talk, then the guy glanced back at me in my Bronco. The guard walked back into the building, and the arm blocking our path lifted a moment later. Steve pulled ahead, and we entered the subdivision. A couple of rights and lefts later, Steve pulled nose-in into a parking spot designated for visitors. I did the same a couple of spots down. By the time I got out of my truck, Steve was walking my way.

"Up here and across the street," he said. "Maybe four or five houses down."

"Sure," I said.

We walked down the sidewalk toward the address. I took the homes in as we did. The neighborhood reminded me of Steve's. Each house—single-family and probably around twenty-five hundred square feet—looked damn close in appearance to the next, minus some small details and colors. They were all two stories, with two-car garages, and sat on small lots with perfectly edged lawns. Each lot featured one palm tree and some small but meticulous landscaping. Each house had a terra-cotta tile roof. Through the twenty-foot gaps between the houses, I could see that man-made canals ran through the backyards.

"Here we go," Steve said. He pointed at the house we sought and crossed the pavered street toward it. The house looked like every other one in the neighborhood. No cars were in the driveway. We walked to the front door, and Steve gave it a rap with his knuckles. A dog barked.

"What were the parents' names?" I asked.

"Patrick on who we figure to be the father. Megan's the mother."

I nodded.

A moment later, a woman opened the front door. "Hello," she said. She looked Steve and me up and down and slouched a bit.

The woman, in her forties, had shoulder-length brown hair. She was dressed in jeans and a white blouse.

"Ma'am," I said, "are you Megan Bowe?"

"I am. And you're the police," she said.

"Lieutenant Harrington and Sergeant Steve Walsh," I said.

"I'm guessing this has something to do with my daughter Kylie. She doesn't live here."

The little doubt that we were dealing with Kylie Bowe's parents vanished.

"We're aware of that, ma'am," Steve said.

"Then what are you…" Her sentence trailed off. The woman pulled in a couple of quick erratic breaths, as if she was expecting the news that we were about to deliver. "Is she…?"

"We're sorry, Mrs. Bowe," I said. "Her body was found this morning."

The woman covered her mouth with her hand. Her emotions overtook her, and her knees buckled. Megan Bowe slid down the home's open front door and collapsed on the wood floor inside the doorway.

"Mom, what's going on?" I heard.

I glanced up to see a young woman walking toward us from the kitchen area at the rear of the house, and she looked like the spitting image of Kylie Bowe.

CHAPTER 9

Prior to leaving, we told Megan Bowe that her daughter had been murdered. We left her with our cards and Skip's information. I asked Mrs. Bowe to call us as soon as she felt ready so we could interview her and her family.

Steve and I got back to the station around three o'clock. I headed downstairs to the crime lab to see what if anything Colt and the guys had come up with. I found Colt inside one of the glass labs at the computer. I gave the door a knock, and he waved me in. I saw what had to have been Kylie Bowe's outfit on the table in the center of the room. It was laid out just as it would have been worn—shirt on top and then belt and skirt. Her knee-high boots sat below the skirt.

"We have prints and hits," Colt said. He ran his hand through his long blond hair and pointed at his computer monitor. "I have another set running and was going to call you as soon as I had the results for both." He pushed the office chair next to him toward me.

I took the seat.

"You got the prints from the skirt?" I asked.

"Yup. I'm not sure what the hell the thing is made from.

It's not anything natural. It almost feels like rubber or synthetic plastic or something. There's no tag saying what it actually is. Either way, it's a print magnet."

Colt clicked at his keyboard, and a man's sheet popped up on screen. "Henry Grammer. Fifty-five. Lives in Brownsville. Some priors for DUI. One arrest for what looks like possession with intent in the eighties."

"Nothing violent, though?"

Colt shook his head and turned the computer monitor toward me. He pushed over the mouse, and I scrolled down the page.

"How do I print this?" I asked.

"Just hit control P," he said. "It will give you a printable page version."

I did, then I grabbed the guy's sheet from the printer at the back of the lab. "When do you think we'll know on the other prints?"

"It's been running them for quite a bit now," Colt said. "That usually means we aren't getting a hit."

"What about those fingernail scrapings?" I asked.

"They'll be what I start on after I finish up with the prints and clothing. I still need to look for trace, plus I haven't even got to the boots yet."

"Okay," I said. "Did you get anything from Skip?"

"Not yet," Colt said. "He was getting started with the autopsy when I spoke to him earlier. Once he was finished up with that, he said he was going to take some high-res photos of the wrist area where the hand was removed. He's going to have to take a mold of the bone so we can try to match up the cut with a tool that did it."

"Where are all the photos from this morning?" I asked.

"I have Gomez developing them as we speak."

"All right. When they're done, can you make sure I get all of them in a file on my desk? I'd like to go through them again."

"We'll get you some copies, sure," he said.

"Okay," I said. I flicked the guy's rap sheet with my finger. "I'm going to run with this guy and see what we get. Let me know when you get an answer on those."

"Will do."

I left Colt's lab and went upstairs to my office. I wanted to see which precinct oversaw that area. I brought up the address, and it was within a stone's throw of the Miami Springs PD, which wasn't a part of the Miami-Dade PD as most of us were. I dialed their station and rocked back in my office chair. After going through a couple of prompts, I got someone on the line.

"Miami Springs Police," a woman answered.

"Hello. This is Lieutenant Nash Harrington from Miami Homicide. I'm actually looking to speak with someone in Patrol."

"Regarding?" she asked.

"I've got a person of interest out in your area. I'd like to see if maybe an officer could drive past his residence and pick him up for me."

"Give me one second, Lieutenant. I'm going to put you through to the patrol sergeant's desk."

"Thank you," I said.

A moment later, a sergeant by the name of Barshop came on the phone. I filled him in on what we had going on, and he agreed to send someone by the house to try to pick up Grammer. I thanked him and left him with my contact information. If they located our guy, they'd call, he said.

"How's it coming?" Halloway asked.

I looked up to see him leaning against my open doorway. I rocked my head back and forth. "A couple of trails to start down."

"Anything further on the missing hand?" he asked.

"Unfortunately, no," I said.

"You know, I was trying to kick around some ideas."

"On the hand?" I asked.

"Yeah. Reasons why you'd chop off a prostitute's hand."

"As opposed to *we have some kind of nut killing people and keeping their hands as trophies.*"

"Exactly," he said.

"Understandable," I said. "What did you come up with?"

"Maybe she scratched our killer," Halloway said. "Clawed him up. That seems a likely scenario to me, especially considering the cause of death. A woman being strangled is going to kick and swat. Swiping and scratching at her assailant's face and arms seems pretty logical to me."

"Colt took a scraping from her left hand," I said. "It's a logical reason, but could our killer, in the middle of strangling someone, really be sure he was scratched with just one hand and certain that he wasn't touched with the other? I'd think if they were going to go through with the hassle of chopping off one of her hands, they'd take both just in case."

"You're probably right. What about tattoos? Maybe she had an identifiable tattoo on her hand," the captain said.

"Possibility," I said. "I guess we didn't bother asking anyone about that. We had her ID pretty much right away, though."

"That still could be a reason for doing it," he said.

"It could. I'll ask the next person that I talk to who would know. What else?" I asked.

"Those were my two big ones," he said.

"Maybe we'll find out when we have the person responsible linked up."

Halloway gave me a nod. "Are you going to stay the rest of the afternoon?"

"May as well," I said. "Not much point in going home now. Only about two hours until my shift would normally end, anyway."

"If you ever left when it did."

I shrugged.

"Take a day off when we wrap this up. Leave your phone turned off," he said.

"Sure," I said.

I imagined we both knew that I wouldn't be doing either. My desk phone rang.

As I reached for it, the captain said we'd talk later and left my office. I brought my phone to my ear. "Harrington."

"Um, hello. This is Selma Bowe. Kylie's sister."

The woman's voice sounded faint—just above a whisper. I heard her sniff.

"My mother gave me your information."

Kylie's sister had heard Steve and me speaking with her mother when we were at the house. She knew that Kylie had been murdered.

"Hello, Ms. Bowe," I said. "We're sorry about your sister."

She sniffed again. "Thank you. My mom said you had questions about Kylie?"

"We just wanted to ask your family some things about her so we could maybe get a better picture of her life. The more we know about her, the better our chances can be of finding who did this."

"My parents hadn't talked to her in almost a year. Probably longer before that," she said. "They gave up on her."

"All right. You kept in contact with her, though?"

"A little. I tried. When she wasn't high on something, we would still talk. I'd drive down to that house she was living in and try to take her out to lunch every now and then. Sometimes, when Coolie wasn't around, she'd come. Sometimes she was too messed up. Sometimes she would be beat up—black eyes and bruises. Bad dates, she would say."

Selma filled me in on Kylie's drug use, which started in her early teens. She spoke about her parents sticking Kylie in one treatment facility after another. Selma talked about finding her sister overdosed and covered in vomit in her bedroom. How Kylie disappeared at sixteen and was found in a crack-house raid three months later. She spoke of her friends talking about seeing her sister working a corner. Nothing she said sounded good.

While I was getting a clearer picture of Kylie and her life, none of it was getting us closer to a suspect. None of it was giving us a place to start. I asked Selma if she could think of anyone who would do that to her sister, but she came up blank. I asked if she thought Leon Reese—or Coolie, as he was known—or Michelle Dirol could have been responsible. Selma didn't think any of her sister's housemates were capable. I asked when was the last time she'd seen or spoken to her sister, and she said weeks.

The three hours I remained at the station didn't get us any further ahead. Barshop, the sergeant from the Miami Springs PD, called me back around four thirty. The cars that reported to the home of Henry Grammer, the man whom we'd received a fingerprint hit on, found themselves a locked door and no one home. The neighbors that Barshop's officers spoke to said they'd seen him leave earlier in the day. Barshop ended our call by saying that his guys would keep their eyes open and try Grammer's house later that night and again in the morning.

The second set of prints returned no results. They weren't in the system. I locked up my office and headed home around six.

CHAPTER 10

Clifford had found his desired area of town—Liberty City. He'd even found his targets. While driving from one city block to the next, he'd seen a couple of potential candidates, but the perfect ones were the three men who had never left one corner over the course of a couple of hours. Clifford had parked two blocks down on a side street, but from his corner he had a view of the men through his binoculars. One of the guys was on the corner, lit by the streetlight above him. Another man appeared to be on lookout duty, while the third was at the window of a parked car. Neighborhood drug dealers. Clifford was certain they were armed and certain they were the perfect targets.

He snugged the side straps on his vest and double-checked his gear—two custom-made Springfield Armory 1911s and two extra magazines for each. He racked the slide on each pistol and placed them in the vest's built-in holsters under each arm. A loop of Velcro fastener on the front of his body armor waited to accept his hatchet that he'd put on the moment he stepped from the car. Clifford was well aware that his truck stuck out like a sore thumb and figured it wouldn't make the best getaway vehicle. He needed something that would blend in, to make him almost unnoticeable. He rented a midsized sedan in a boring gold color.

Clifford could see the car that was purchasing whatever drugs they were peddling pull away from the men. It was time. He took a couple of quick breaths and strapped the ballistic mask to his face. Through the eyeholes in the black mask, he got a look at himself in the car's side mirror—menacing, he thought.

Clifford reached over to the passenger seat, scooped up his hatchet, then pulled the door handle. He stepped into the street and secured the hatchet to his vest. He walked down the sidewalk to the men. When he was fifty feet away, the man closest to him spotted him.

"What the hell is this?" the guy said. "This guy thinks it's Halloween."

The other two men turned their attention to Clifford. He continued his pace.

He saw the guy that had been looking out on the corner, and closest to him, reach for his waistline.

The man lifted his basketball jersey and pointed at his pistol tucked into the waist of his baggy shorts. "You came to the right place if you're looking for trouble," the guy said.

Clifford crossed his arms over his chest and grasped the handles of the pistols he had holstered under his arms. He drew them and walked forward with both guns out before him.

The guy pulled his gun from his waistline and spouted off some tough talk as he emphasized his words with his weapon. Clifford saw the guy holding the gun in a sideways grip, like most would-be criminals and gangsters from television and film. Clifford wasn't too worried that the guy would even hit him if he did get off a shot.

Clifford fired three times. The cracks from the rounds broke the night air. The guy that was talking tough and waving his gun in the air dropped to his knees. His gun didn't leave his grip. Clifford continued to advance. The man he'd shot was ten feet away. Clifford put another pair of rounds into him but didn't take his eyes from the other two men holding their ground thirty feet away. He thought the guys would run. They didn't. Both had their weapons drawn.

Clifford aimed a gun on each man before him. He saw the muzzle flash of one of the man's weapons and felt a crack to his forehead, as if he'd been punched. The shot had to have barely grazed his mask. A direct shot would have still put him to the ground. Before he could return fire, the echo of automatic gunfire rang in his ears. Clifford went to the ground as he returned fire on the two men. He'd been hit, and in multiple places. Clifford saw the man with the automatic drop. Through the holes of his ballistic mask, his eyes shot to the other man advancing with his gun outstretched. Clifford fired several times. The man's body jerked from the rounds entering him. He saw the guy's head snap backward violently. His body dropped to the ground, lifeless.

Clifford groaned as he pushed off from the ground and stood. He tried getting a look at himself for damage, to see if any of the rounds he'd taken had gone through his armor. He saw no blood. While he understood he'd taken multiple rounds, he couldn't pinpoint a single place that felt as he'd imagined a bullet wound would feel—not that he knew from being shot by a gun before. Clifford looked up. His eyes went from one man to the next. The two nearer him weren't moving. The guy who'd sprayed him with the automatic weapon was pulling himself across the sidewalk, trying to get away. Clifford swapped a magazine into his weapon that was empty. He tucked the empty magazine into his body armor and walked to the guy who was still alive.

"Hey!" Clifford heard. "What the hell is going on out here?"

Another person screamed.

He heard someone else shout.

His head snapped to the left. People had come from the front of their homes. He imagined the sound of gunfire would only bring out more of the neighborhood to see what was going on. He needed them to disperse. Clifford turned his weapon on the people who'd gathered and fired a few rounds, not trying to hit them but trying to get them to retreat into their homes. A few of his rounds bounced off the street, and some plugged into the grass of the front yards. The people who were outside ducked and scrambled away from the houses.

Clifford's attention returned to the guy who'd been retreating, or at least attempting to. A bloody drag mark stretched only about ten feet from where he'd started. Clifford stood above him and drew aim on the man's back.

He fired three rounds into him. The guy stopped moving and went facedown on the sidewalk. Clifford holstered his weapons and pulled his hatchet from the Velcro loop securing it. He crouched beside the man. The guy's left arm was out before him. Clifford took aim with the hatchet and, with three swings, removed the guy's hand from his wrist. He stayed crouched and fished a small plastic bag from his pocket. As Clifford began to place the hand inside the bag, he again heard shouting. Someone was calling out to him. Clifford glanced over his shoulder, and a man armed with a shotgun was crossing the street toward him.

Clifford immediately dropped the bagged hand and ripped both of his firearms from their holsters. He stood, spun around, and took his aim. The man had the shotgun in his shoulder, just thirty feet away. Clifford squeezed the triggers of his weapons but saw the air in front of the advancing man light up in a fireball. The impact of the shot sent Clifford backward and to the ground. He couldn't get a breath. His left armed burned like nothing he'd ever felt. Through the holes in his mask, Clifford could see the guy down in the middle of the street. Behind the ringing in his ears from the shotgun blast, he could hear more people screaming and shouting. Clifford's breath returned. He stood and again fired on the man in the street, hitting him multiple times.

Two men screamed at him from a front porch, and a woman wailed. Clifford snatched the bagged hand from the ground and started in the direction of his rental car.

"Don't let him get away," someone shouted—a woman's

voice. Clifford stopped in the street, a half block from his car. He brought both weapons up and took his aim on the people on their porches. They ducked, and some ran. Clifford began firing. He'd get away unseen if he had to kill every person in the neighborhood.

CHAPTER 11

The sound of my chirping and vibrating phone woke me. It took a moment for my eyes to focus. Not a hint of daylight came into my bedroom windows.

I reached over for my phone, which was lighting up the room. The screen said it was Dave, and the time was 5:10 a.m.

I clicked Talk and brought the phone to my ear. "Yeah, Dave. What's up?"

"Sorry it's so early. I kind of figured that you'd want to hear about this right away. We've got a mess here."

"Hold on," I said. I kicked my legs out from the covers and out of bed. I pulled on a pair of shorts and left the bedroom. Lucky, who'd been wakened by my movements, followed me. I walked the hall and made a left into the kitchen. After sliding open the patio doors to let the dog out, I went back to the call.

"All right. What the hell is going on?" I asked. I scooted up onto the kitchen counter.

"We're at the scene of a damn shootout in Liberty City," he said.

"Who's we?" I asked.

"About twenty guys from Patrol, me, Burns, Malone, the crime lab, ambulances, and a couple of news vans."

"All right. All right. What do we know?" I asked.

"I know that we probably have fifty or more shots fired. We have five DBs on scene. We have another two with gunshots that the EMTs are attending to. And I know that we have one DB that is missing one of his damn hands."

"Missing a hand?" I asked.

"Yeah. With a witness that says she saw the hand get removed with a hatchet."

"So, someone saw our killer?" I asked.

"About ten people did," Dave said. "Maybe more. The guy was dressed in black, head to toe. Like a SWAT guy with a black mask, one of the witnesses said. A couple people said that he was bullet proof, that he got shot a bunch of times and kept going. One person said they saw the guy get shot in the face and then get mowed down by an automatic weapon before standing back up and opening up on those who'd shot him. The woman who said he chopped off the one guy's hand said he took a shotgun blast from maybe twenty feet."

"Okay. So, he is either superhuman or was wearing some serious body armor. Tell me about the removal of the hand," I said.

"He crouched beside one of the men he'd shot and chopped it off."

"Taken from the scene?" I asked.

"Yeah, no sign of the hand," Dave said.

"And all this happened when the neighborhood was, what, outside in the streets watching?"

"The gunfire brought people from their homes. He fired on the gathered homeowners multiple times. Four homeowners were hit. Two dead and two at the hospital. One of the deceased was an older woman. The other deceased was the guy who fired on our shooter with the shotgun. He was killed in the street."

I dug my fingers into my eyes. "What did we get as far as a description of the guy other than dressed in black with a mask?"

"Average height and weight. That's really it."

"Race?" I asked.

"Unknown. He was covered literally from head to toe. Gloves, a black pullover head covering beneath the mask."

"What do we know about the mask?" I asked.

"One guy said it kind of looked like a hockey mask."

"It wasn't a hockey mask if he took a shot to it," I said.

"Agreed. Ballistics mask, maybe," Dave said. "We have a woman who says that she saw him leave in a car—she can't say make or model or plate or color."

"So, useless," I said.

"She didn't say truck," Dave said.

"True."

"Hang on a sec, Harrington." I heard him talking to someone on his end of the call. "Hey, we have a couple more witnesses coming out of the woodwork here. I'm going to go give the guys a hand. Are you coming down, or did you just want to catch up when your shift starts? I imagine this is going to be all over the damn news and an all-hands-on-deck, around-the-clock kind of a thing."

I let out a big breath. The thought of another two hours of sleep was nice, yet I knew it wouldn't happen. I'd lie there for maybe a half hour at the most before getting up, getting ready, then leaving for the scene, pissed off that I wasted a half hour. "I'm getting ready now," I said. "Text me the address."

He did, and I attempted to get ready without waking Amy. It was her day off, and she'd mentioned wanting to sleep in. I grabbed everything I needed from the bedroom and made my way to the guest bathroom to shower and get ready. The second I stepped a foot into the shower, I heard the door open and Amy ask what I was doing.

I pulled the curtain open and looked out at Amy, who was leaning against the wall. She yawned into her hand.

"I was trying not to wake you up," I said. "Guess that didn't work out too hot."

"I thought I dreamed that work called you, and then I woke up and heard the shower kick on in here."

"Dave called. We have some shit going down in Liberty City. A shootout. A couple of DBs."

"Let me go make you some coffee," she said.

"Go back to bed. You don't have to do that."

"It's okay," she said. "I'll be going back to bed the second you leave and probably won't even remember being up. Did you feed the dog?"

"Not yet," I said.

"Okay." Amy left the bathroom.

I was showered and dressed inside of ten minutes. As I

was pulling my shoulder holster on, I kept smelling food.

I walked into the kitchen to the sound of a sizzling pan. Lucky, sitting in the center of the kitchen, glanced at me for a split second then went back to observing Amy at the stove. My eyes went to the countertop where Amy stood. I saw a travel cup of coffee and a plate with a green mound on it. A glass of orange juice sat next to the plate. Amy slid two eggs from the pan onto what I could only assume was either lettuce or spinach. She glanced over her shoulder at me.

"Making yourself some breakfast?" I asked.

She leaned forward, set the pan down, and clicked off the burner. Amy scooped up the plate and juice and walked them to the table. "I made you some breakfast. Eat."

"Babe, I have to go," I said.

"Eat," she said. "I know you. You won't eat until lunch, which will be some greasy fast food or something from the vending machines at work. Take two minutes and eat something that's not awful."

I glanced at the plate, spotting some sliced-up cherry tomatoes and a few random bacon chunks mixed in to what I confirmed to be a bed of lettuce beneath the eggs. A handful of croutons sat off to the side. "Salad for breakfast?"

"It's a BLT salad with an egg. Eat it. You'll like it," she said.

When I thought of a BLT, there was no salad involved. My BLTs were on some thick white bread with some big tomato slices, a pile of bacon, maybe one or two pieces of lettuce, and a bunch of mayo. I sat at the table and looked down at what sat before me. I knew I wouldn't get out of the house without eating it, so I grabbed the fork and started in. Surprisingly, it wasn't as awful as I would have thought.

"Well?" she asked.

I downed my juice and speared another forkful of egg and arugula. "I guess it's passable as food."

"Passable as food?" She crossed her arms over her chest.

"Okay, okay. It's actually pretty decent."

"That's better. See, not everything has to be soaked in butter." Amy grabbed my coffee in my travel mug and set it down beside me. She kissed my cheek as I sat in my chair. "Have a good day. Be safe. Call me when you can. Love you."

"Love you too," I said.

I finished the rest of my breakfast-salad deal and was out the door with my travel mug of coffee. The sun wouldn't be up for another two hours. The air was damp, and the temperature was somewhere in the seventies—a standard late-spring Miami morning. I jumped into the Bronco, set my coffee in the cup holder, and made my way toward Liberty City.

CHAPTER 12

The drive, traffic free at that time in the morning, took me just twenty minutes. I pulled up to the scene right around six. The better part of the city block was lit up like daylight from the news vans' lights. I didn't bother to weave through the cruisers, ambulances, and coroners' vans clogging the street. Just beyond where they were all parked, I could see a string of yellow police tape ahead, stretching from a light pole on one side of the street to another light pole on the other. I parked the Bronco behind the last patrol car in line on the right-hand side of the road and stepped from my car. Uniformed officers milled about. The homes of the neighborhood were small, probably sixty-plus years old and less than a thousand square feet. Most sat behind waist-high chain-link fences. To my left was a crowd of about ten people gathered on the sidewalk and staring over at the scene—neighborhood residents, I imagined. There was another group of equal size off to my right. While I could see a couple of reporters doing their thing in front of cameras, it appeared that the officers on scene had done a good job of keeping the media back.

I walked past an ambulance and a few patrol cars to the police tape, where I was immediately met by a pair of officers.

"Lieutenant Harrington, Miami Homicide," I said. I pulled my shield from my hip and held it up.

"Sure, Lieutenant," one of the officers said. "All the way up the block." He pointed up the street. "Most everything happened at the intersection there."

I looked in the direction where he'd pointed. Under the streetlights of the T intersection, more officers walked the street, and a couple of bodies had blue tarps over them. I dipped under the tape and started walking to everyone. Closest to me were some of our crime lab guys —Craig Town, the night shift crime lab lead, and Buckley, his Mohawk-sporting assistant. Within ten yards of the guys, I spotted shell casings all over the ground.

"Morning, guys," I said.

"Lieutenant," Craig said.

Buckley gave me a nod and went back to snapping photos.

I stopped beside them. Craig was setting evidence cones around some of the spent casings.

"Our shooters?" I asked.

"Yeah, forty-five caliber rounds. Aside from that, there is some blood mixed in with the spent rounds."

"Our guy got hit, huh?"

"It would appear so. All the casings are right here, which is consistent with the story we got of him firing on the homeowners from this area. The blood heads in that direction, where we believe he had a car parked." He pointed. "We're headed that way as soon as we get everything here marked."

"Okay. Do you know where Ramirez is?"

"The corner there," Craig said. He nodded at the corner of the T intersection.

"All right. I'll check back with you guys in a bit." I started toward Dave, who was standing under a streetlight and talking with some uniformed officers. On the other side of the street, Dave's detectives, Malone and Burns, were speaking with a man who appeared to be somewhere in his sixties, judging by his white hair and beard.

As I walked toward him, Dave waved me over. The officers Dave was talking to dispersed as I neared.

"Just get here?" Dave asked.

"Yeah. What do we know?"

"Well, we have different parts of the story that we stitched together from different witnesses, but most of it all fits. First, we have the guy over there with Malone and Burns who says he was sitting in his living room watching television when he started to hear shouting outside. He says he looked out the window to see some guy in black with a pair of guns walking straight for the guys on the corner. He said the man was wearing tactical gear from top to bottom. He's the one who gave us the SWAT description. Before the witness even knows what the hell is going on outside his house, he said, the guy in the black gear started shooting. The second that bullets started flying, he got away from his front windows, stayed low, and got to the kitchen."

"So that's all he saw?" I asked.

"Yeah." Dave waved for me to follow him as he spoke

over his shoulder. He pointed at the ground. "We have shell casings all around here. These are forty-five caliber. We figure these to be from our suspect. The four deceased here were all armed yet none with a forty-five." Dave stopped at the first tarped-over body. "Each of these guys have multiple GSWs, and we also have forty-five casings near each body. This guy here was packing a Beretta nine millimeter." Dave crouched and pulled the corner of the tarp back. The man underneath, African-American and in his early twenties, wore a basketball jersey. His pistol lay beside him. "We got names on all of these guys from the people in the neighborhood here. This one is Isiah Muhgabe."

I pulled out my notepad and wrote the name down. "These guys were all carrying?"

"Correct."

"What, were they out here dealing?"

"That's the theory, and we had a couple of the people around here say that's what was going down. Patrol backs it up. Seems that some of the officers were familiar with our victims. I'd imagine when the bodies are searched, we find drugs ready for sale."

"I don't imagine that a drug deal gone wrong would account for someone showing up in armor and then taking a hand when he left," I said.

"I doubt it," Dave said. "Whoever did this had some big ol' brass balls, though. This generally isn't the neighborhood to come into and just start shooting."

"That's putting it lightly," I said. "Do we have IDs on everyone?"

"All of them, yes."

"Okay. What's with these two guys?" I pointed two fingers at the other two tarps that sat twenty feet up the sidewalk. Dave started walking to them.

"Vics two and three," Dave said. "This is Kenyan Miller. He took a couple to the body and a head shot. It looks like he was packing a three eighty—some kind of older pistol. Every marking was filed from it. A throwaway if I ever saw one. Need to see the body."

I reluctantly took a quick look. Mr. Miller looked similar in age to the first vic. He had an entrance wound below his right eye that was making it sag a bit. I didn't need to see anything else and sure as hell didn't need to see the exit wound. Dave let the tarp drop, and we moved to the third man. About ten feet from the tarp, I spotted on the ground a MAC-10, or some variant of the weapon, and what looked like bloody drag marks to the point where the tarp was.

"I'm assuming the gun there was responsible for the report of automatic fire," Dave said. "And witnesses say our suspect took the rounds. Everything is filed off the gun, but judging by the casings all over the ground, it's a nine-millimeter version."

"And our suspect took rounds from it?" I asked.

"That's what the witnesses say," Dave said. "Our female witness who is giving her statement to Chestnut"—Dave flipped his notebook back a page or two—"Annette Williams. Netty, she goes by. She said that the sound of the first shots brought her to her door. She said she saw our suspect and these two guys exchanging fire from maybe twenty feet from each other. The suspect fell from the shots but then got back up." Dave tucked his notepad back into the inner pocket of his black suit jacket.

"Any blood found over here?" I asked. "That we can attribute to someone other than the deceased?"

"Not here on the sidewalk, but the crime lab boys got some back there in the street."

"Yeah, I talked to them when I walked up. Okay. So, he takes fire and then gets up," I said.

"Yeah. And turns his gun on the people who came from their houses. The Annette woman said he fired a couple of times at the people who'd gathered. She took cover inside but immediately returned to the window." Dave crouched beside the body of the third man and pulled the tarp back. "She said when she returned to the window, this guy was dragging himself away. The suspect stood over him and fired a couple more shots into the guy. Then he holstered his weapons and took out the hatchet. She said she saw him chopping away. Removing the hand."

"This guy's name?" I asked.

"LaShawn Robinson."

I got a look at the man beneath the tarp. He was facedown. His shirt, which once was white, was completely red with blood. His right and left arms were out to his sides and above his head. I imagined they remained in the position they were in when he'd been dragging himself across the sidewalk. His left hand was gone, and a pool of blood stemmed from his wrist.

I let out a big breath and turned back toward the homes

on the far side of the street. They were maybe thirty yards away. Even without the lighting from the news vans, the streetlights themselves would have provided plenty of illumination for the witnesses to get a good look at what happened. My eyes went to the tarp in the center of the street.

Dave must have seen me put eyes on it.

"That's the neighbor, Ben Hensley. Age fifty-six. He came out of his house and across the street with a shotgun. The Netty woman said that he fired on our suspect, putting him to the ground, before he again rose and returned fire. After killing the neighbor in the street, our suspect retreated south and stopped in the middle of the street to fire on the residents who'd gathered again."

I started walking toward the body of Mr. Hensley in the street. Dave was following me. "Which house did this guy live in?" I asked over my shoulder.

"That one there," Dave said. He pointed at the small tan-colored single story with the lights on inside.

"Does anyone else live at the house?" I asked.

Dave shook his head. "The people we spoke with said he lived alone."

I looked down at the shotgun in the street. "Do we know what kind of rounds were in this thing?"

"Haven't checked," Dave said. "But after hearing he's been shot, multiple times it appears, and the guys finding blood, we already spread the word to local medical facilities."

"You'd have to think, body armor or not, taking a round of anything out of a shotgun at that kind of distance is going to put a damper on your day."

"One would think," Dave said.

"Where is the last victim?" I asked.

Dave pointed two houses up the block. "Female, sixties. Eleanor Vasquez. She came out of the house, like about everyone else in the neighborhood, to see what happened. When he turned his fire to those who'd gathered, she took a pair of rounds in the back."

I jammed my fingers in my eyes for a hard rub. I looked in the direction that I'd come from, where Town and Buckley had found the shooter's blood. Behind the patrol cars, their flashing lights and the ambulance, I couldn't see the people that I had passed walking up to the scene, but I imagined they were all still there. If our shooter fled in that direction, they were the people who I wanted to talk to.

CHAPTER 13

Clifford sat on his bathroom vanity. He needed the mirror as he worked. His shirt was off, and blood covered his arm. He gritted his teeth and pulled the dental floss, which he'd tied to a sewing needle, through his flesh. He imagined that sewing himself up would have hurt worse if it wasn't for the combination of adrenaline and painkillers.

The man had fired a shell of buckshot at him from not much more than twenty feet. Clifford had thought himself lucky that he still had an arm at all and wasn't dead. His body armor had caught most of it, yet a single pellet had passed through his flesh. The pellet had passed through Clifford's left arm just above his elbow in the area of his lower triceps. The skin had completely torn, leaving him with a nasty flesh wound about a good inch and a half deep and three inches long. Thankfully, nothing had hit bone. While the blood loss and wound was still significant, Clifford didn't think that an artery or anything vital was hit. His plan was to sew himself up, eat antibiotics and painkillers over the next week, and see how things went. Worst-case scenario, he could take a trip south of the border and get real medical attention if necessary.

As Clifford inserted the needle, popped it through the other side of his flesh, and pulled each suture tight, he thought about having taken the men out. While he'd received return fire, they were still overmatched. The men simply weren't on his level. Clifford guessed that it had come down to training and hardware. The men couldn't aim. They fired blindly with inferior weapons. They had no protection. If he really wanted to test his might, he'd need to select a more formidable adversary. Someone more prepared.

CHAPTER 14

Dave had Burns and Malone work the groups of people who had gathered. Up to that point, it seemed as if everyone was trying to get a look at the scene and hadn't actually witnessed anything.

I'd interviewed Greg Coleman, the man who had been watching television when he saw our shooter approach. I didn't get much more than what the man told Dave he had seen. It seemed as soon as the shooting began, Mr. Coleman hit the deck and retreated to the far end of his home, where he remained until well after the shooting stopped. The guy also didn't add much to the description of "a man dressed in SWAT gear," which I took to mean top-to-bottom body armor. After talking with Mr. Coleman, I spoke with a couple of the other neighbors reported to have been in the crowd that took fire. Most of them had the same story—they gathered to see what the hell was going on, saw the shooting of one or more of the men, depending on when they arrived at the group, then saw the shooter turn the gun on the crowd. After all the people we talked to, our description didn't get much better than the shooter's average height and weight, black clothing, black mask. We didn't have a race. We didn't have a vehicle.

Colt was on the scene by seven o'clock. He'd said that Town had called him with a few questions, and as soon as Colt heard what went down, he was on his way in. With the number of shots fired, multiple bodies, and the amount of blood evidence, the crime lab would probably need to spend the better part of the day on location.

The time was inching up on eight. I'd given my team a call and doled out some instructions. Steve and Ryan would meet me on scene, and Garcia was to head to Jackson Memorial Hospital. I'd given him the names of the two people who had been shot and taken there by the EMTs. The word was that neither had life-threatening injuries. I wanted Garcia to get their accounts of what happened as soon as we could.

Two of the three men that we figured to be our drug dealers—LaShawn Robinson and Kenyan Miller—did in fact have packaged drugs on their person. After the drugs had been tested, photographed, and booked with the rest of the evidence, Colt gave Skip and his team from the county medical examiner's office permission to take the bodies. Skip had said that he would remove the rounds from the victims and get them to Colt and the crime lab to start on the bullet ballistics reports as soon as he could.

I stood in the bright purple kitchen of Annette Williams's home. The floor was black-and-white-checkered linoleum, which matched the checkered pattern of the countertops and backsplash. The curtains over the window by the sink were bright purple. The round kitchen table where she sat had a bright yellow tablecloth.

Dave sat at the table along with Chestnut. The guys had asked Mrs. Williams to draw on a piece of paper what the man's mask looked like. She drew an oval with a pair of eyeholes.

"Mrs. Williams, can you think of anything that would make this man recognizable?" I asked. "Did he have a limp? Walk funny? See any hair sticking out of his hood or mask? Recognize his shoes? Anything?"

Annette Williams was a heavyset fifty-some-year-old woman. She sat at her kitchen table, chain-smoking cigarettes. In between puffs, she'd sniff. I noticed her hand tremble each time she ashed a cigarette in the ashtray before her. She seemed pretty shaken up about what happened. She simply said no to my questions.

Dave turned in his chair and glanced at me. "I think we're good."

We'd been in the woman's house for a solid half hour, and she really hadn't given us anything. Further questioning regarding the man's outfit netted us nothing more than what we already knew. We had her statement, so moving on was probably our best bet. We thanked her for her time, left her with our information, and walked from the front of her home. Light had just broken about forty-five minutes earlier. In the time that we'd been in the woman's house, the scene out front had fewer patrol cars and officers but more people from the community—and more news vans.

Burns and Malone were walking down the sidewalk toward us. "We have a camera," Burns said.

"Where?" Dave asked.

"A half block up."

Dave, Chestnut, and I passed through the chain-link gate at the front of Annette Williams's fence and met the detectives at the sidewalk.

"What's on the footage?" I asked.

"Don't know. No one answers at the door," Malone said. "But there is a camera pointed at the street. Red light lit."

"Let's do what we can about finding out who lives there and how we can look at what they got," Dave said.

"I'll go pull the address up in the car. Give me a second," Burns said. He walked to a line of unmarked cruisers parked on Thirteenth.

"Let's hope the damn thing isn't a dummy," I said. "And actually caught something."

I felt my phone vibrating in my pocket. I yanked it out, caught a number on the screen that I didn't recognize, and hit Talk as I took a couple of steps away from the guys on the sidewalk. "Lieutenant Harrington."

"Lieutenant. Sergeant Barshop, Miami Springs PD."

"Sergeant," I said. "Any news?"

"We have your guy. Picked him up around an hour ago at his house."

"Is he injured?" I asked.

"He doesn't appear to be. Should he be?"

"Did he have an account of his whereabouts overnight?" I asked.

"We didn't ask. Did you need us to ask him some questions?"

I thought about asking him to run a few preliminary

questions by the guy they'd picked up, but at that point, he was our best lead, and I wanted to handle the interrogation myself.

"Nah. Just hang on to him for a bit. I'm going to turn this scene I'm on over to my sergeant when he arrives, then I'll be over to your station to interview him."

"All right," he said.

"Should I just ask for you at the front?"

"That's fine. How long are you thinking?"

I glanced over at the reporters, whose number continued to grow. "Should be within the hour."

"Not a problem."

I clicked off from the call and immediately dialed Steve. When I'd talked to him a half hour prior, he said he was hopping in the shower and heading out.

"I'm pulling in behind your shitbox as we speak," Steve answered.

"You mean Bronco," I said.

"No. I'm pretty sure it's yours," he said.

"Whatever. I just needed an ETA, but you're here. We're right here inside of the tape. You can't miss us."

"Be there in a second."

I clicked off from the call and walked back to Malone, Chestnut, and Dave.

"I just got a call from Miami Springs PD. They picked up the guy that we had a hit on prints from," I said.

"The ones Colt got from the prostitute's skirt or whatever?" Dave asked.

"Yeah," I said. "How long were you sticking around?"

Dave looked at his watch. "Damn, I didn't know it was this late. As soon as you're ready to take it, we'll probably roll."

"Okay. Did you talk to the press at all?" I asked. "Or did you want me to give them something?"

"Chestnut stepped in front of the bright lights a little earlier. I honestly don't think we have anything further for them," Dave said.

"All right. I'll talk with the captain, and maybe we'll put something together for later today."

Burns crossed the street toward us. He held a small notepad and looked at it as he took a spot next to Dave. "A Shawn Hart is the only thing we can find at the address," Burns said. "Age forty-eight. No priors. Registered vehicle is a couple-year-old Dodge truck."

"There wasn't any truck parked at the street or out front or in the little driveway there," Malone said.

"No, there wasn't," Burns said.

"Okay. We'll have to just keep eyes on the place and check back. Make sure Steve gets that information." I glanced toward the police tape marking our scene and saw Steve showing his credentials to a couple of uniformed officers holding the line. "He's with us!" I called over.

Steve ducked under the tape a second later and approached.

"Morning," he said.

The guys went through their hellos.

"I'm going to turn this scene here over to you, Steve," I said. "Dave is going to bring you up to speed."

"All right," Steve said. "What's going on?"

"I need to shoot over to the Miami Springs station. They picked up the guy who we got the prints on."

"That Colt got last night?" he asked.

"Yeah. They have the guy at their station. Just picked him up."

"What's he saying?"

"They haven't asked him anything," I said. "But from what the sergeant said, he isn't injured and we're pretty certain that our shooter was."

"Are we thinking he may be connected to both the prostitute and what went down there?"

"The missing hand is our only real connection. His prints are on Kylie Bowe's body with a missing hand. It's all we have right now."

"All right. What's going on with Garcia or Ryan?" Steve asked.

"Ryan should be here any minute. I asked Garcia to head over to Jackson Memorial. The two that were shot from here were taken there via ambulance. From what I was told by the EMTs, neither had life-threatening injuries, so I wanted someone there in hopes of getting the two victims interviewed sooner rather than later." I started walking toward the police line. "Call me with an update. I'll do the same."

CHAPTER 15

I pulled into the small parking lot of the Miami Springs Police Department and killed the Bronco's motor. The two-story building's tan and taupe colors let anyone who passed by know it was built sometime in the nineteen eighties. I hopped out, slammed the truck's door, and walked to the police department's entrance on Park Street. The building, set on the corner of Park Street and Westward Drive, held the city hall and fire and police departments. Even though it housed just about every public service for the area, the building was still smaller than the smallest of our Miami PD patrol buildings.

I walked past the front of the building, which was marked City Hall, and made a left at the corner. The police department entrance was the first door, and the open garage doors of the fire department were beyond it. I pulled open the door of the PD and entered a lobby about the size of a home's foyer. A bench sat on the wall to my right, and three chairs were on the wall to my left. The back wall held a security door and a sliding glass window where a uniformed woman sat. Beyond the woman, I could see two lines of desks and a couple of offices inside.

She slid open the glass. "How can I help you?"

"Lieutenant Harrington, Miami Homicide. I'm here to interview a man that you guys picked up for us. I've been in contact with a Sergeant Barshop."

"One second, Lieutenant," she said. The woman, in her forties with long straight brown hair, scooped up the phone in front of her. She plugged in a few numbers and held it to her ear. I heard her tell whoever was on the other end—Barshop, I figured—that a lieutenant was there for him. She hung the phone on its base a moment later.

"Let me buzz you in," she said.

The secured door buzzed, and I pulled it open. The woman stood and pushed a clipboard toward me on the chest-high counter inside the door. "Just sign in for me," she said.

I did, and before she could point me toward wherever Barshop was, a big bald man in a Miami Springs PD uniform and looking somewhere in his fifties approached. A badge was clipped to his upper left chest. Another was embroidered to his left shirtsleeve.

He extended his hand from five feet away. "Sergeant Mark Barshop," he said.

I shook his hand. "Lieutenant Nash Harrington."

"Need anything or are we waiting on anyone?" Barshop asked.

"Not waiting on anyone, but maybe just a copy of his sheet," I said.

Barshop waved over his shoulder for me to follow him.

He popped into his office for a moment and printed off Grammer's sheet along with his DMV record. Papers in hand, we left his office and walked down a hallway at the back of the main room. "We've got him down here," he said. "He's been on ice in our interview room since we picked him up."

"How did the pickup go?" I asked.

"We knocked on his door and asked him to come to the station to answer some questions," Barshop said. "He asked about what, and we said it was a request from Miami-Dade PD." Barshop and I walked the short hallway, and he swiped a card in a secured door. The lock freed and allowed us into another hallway, white floored and white walled.

"That was it?" I asked.

"From what my officer told me, pretty much. Must not be much of a talker. Or he knew why he was getting picked up." Barshop made a right where the hallway came to a T.

"Did you talk to him at all?" I asked.

"Briefly," Barshop said. "I just told him that someone was on their way to speak with him."

"All right," I said. "What's his demeanor?"

"Calm. He's right up here." Barshop pointed at a pair of doors on the right side of the hall. One said Interview Room, and the other wasn't marked. I figured it was an observation room.

"I'll have to record this," he said. "Policy."

"No worries," I said. "Is the door open or locked from the inside?"

"Open," he said. "Need it locked?"

"Will you be watching?" I asked.

"I'll be sitting in the observation room, yes."

"I should be fine, then. Is he cuffed?"

"No," Barshop said.

"Okay."

Barshop let himself into the observation room, and I entered the interview room. Henry Grammer sat on the left side of a metal desk at the center of the back wall. He looked unkempt and tired. His brown-and-gray hair was long and straggly. He wore some kind of Rastafarian shirt in Jamaican colors. The room itself was cinder block, painted white. The ceiling held four fluorescent lights that buzzed a low hum. "Mr. Grammer," I said. "I'm Lieutenant Harrington from Miami Homicide." I slid out a chair across from him at the desk.

"Homicide?" he asked. "Why does Miami Homicide want to talk to me?" His words were steady. Not a hint of panic, no worry.

I took my seat and had another look at his sheet. His registered vehicle was a couple-year-old black Toyota sedan. His priors were a pair of DUIs and a thirty-year-old possession with intent charge. I set the papers on the desk before me. "Let's start with where you were last night," I said.

"Last night?"

Answering a question with a question was a pretty common stalling tactic. "Yes, last night," I said.

"I was at work. Why?"

"And you work where?" I asked.

"Miami Bottling and Beverage. It's in Medley. In the industrial park there."

I knew the business, and I knew the industrial park. It was only two or three miles from my house. His alibi would be easy to check out.

"What do you do there?" I asked.

"Drive a forklift. Third shift Monday through Friday."

"So, you start work on Sunday, then?" I asked. "Work early Monday morning?"

He shook his head. "No. I start Monday, meaning the first day of my weekly shift is mostly Tuesday morning. Then I work Friday into Saturday."

The hours were different than most third shifts that I was familiar with, but the timeline still had him off work during the early morning hours that Kylie Bowe was killed. I thought about him not being home when Patrol went knocking to pick him up.

"What time do you normally leave for work?" I asked.

"Nine thirty or so. It takes me fifteen or twenty minutes to get there, usually. Can I ask why you asked that?" he asked. "Or why I'm here?"

I deflected his question with one of my own. "But you left before that yesterday," I said.

"Yeah. I went and visited my mother in Hialeah Gardens."

"Do you own any firearms, Mr. Grammer?"

He shook his head. "No."

"Are you injured at all?"

"Injured?" he asked. "I'm fit as a fiddle."

"No wounds that you would have been bleeding from?"

He lifted both hands. "No."

I noticed that he didn't seem to have any problem with his range of motion. He'd lifted his arms and dropped them completely naturally, which meant he more than likely had no wounds to his upper torso.

"You want me to strip so you can check?" he asked. "I can if that's what you're into."

"I don't think that will be necessary. Where were you Sunday night into Monday morning?" I asked.

He paused for a second. The reason he was being interviewed must have dawned on him.

"Why?" he asked. He drew the word out.

"Say, between two in the morning and three or so," I said.

He shook his head. "Look, you're going to tell me why I'm here before I answer anything else. Am I under arrest, or am I free to go, or what?"

I figured I'd get to the point and see what I could get out of him before I made that determination. "We have your prints on a dead prostitute," I said. "She was killed in the early hours of Monday morning."

"What?" he asked.

"Your prints. On a dead woman," I said.

"I, ah, I…" His stammering stopped for a moment. "I didn't kill anyone."

"Right," I said. "Were you in the neighborhood of Biscayne and Seventy-Ninth on Sunday night?"

"Look," he said. He leaned forward in his chair and held up his hands. "Okay. I was there. I picked up a prostitute. I dropped her off right where I found her, alive and well."

"That was where?" I asked.

"Right by the bus stop on Seventy-Ninth. A couple blocks from Biscayne."

"See"—I tapped the metal desk with my fingertip—"here is what I know. I have your prints on a dead prostitute, and you just told me that you were around where she was picked up, and killed, in the time in question. But you're telling me it wasn't you."

"That's exactly what the hell I'm telling you. I dropped her off unharmed and went on my way with a smile on my face."

"What did she look like?"

"Blonde. Early twenties. Attractive. She didn't look like the streets had completely used her up yet."

"Green skirt?" I asked.

He nodded.

"You were in your registered vehicle?" I asked.

"My Camry, yes."

"Anyone who can verify that?" I asked.

He cocked his head as he stared back at me. "I don't really go make sure that I have people lined up to witness me dropping hookers back off where I picked them up."

"Which is where the problem lies," I said.

"You know. Wait. I may have something," he said. "There was another girl on the same corner. I talked to her after I dropped the other one off. The second the girl that was in my car got out, this other one came to my window. Okay looking, bright red hair, unnatural, like brighter than the color of a stop sign. It looked like a dye job and not a wig, though. She was kind of tall. She asked if I could go another round. I made some joke about not being as young as I once was and told her I'd keep eyes open for her the next time I was in the area. She could verify that I dropped the other one off."

"Great," I said. "So, I just need to find a prostitute with bright red hair that remembers your joke and then remembers that you dropped off another prostitute unharmed?"

He didn't respond.

"Excuse me one second, Mr. Grammer." I left the room for the hall. The door of the observation room immediately opened.

Barshop stood in the open doorway. "What are you thinking?"

I shrugged. "Too early to tell." I pulled my phone out and brought up the contact info for the bottling company that he said he worked for. I clicked the prompts on my phone's screen to dial the place's phone number then brought my phone to my ear. "I'm calling now to check on this alibi, though."

"I'm going to bounce over to our lunchroom quick. Did you want something?" he asked.

"I'm good. Appreciate the offer."

He gave me a nod and started down the hall. A ring or two later, someone in the office of the bottling company picked up. I introduced myself to the woman on the line, who transferred me to their personnel manager, a man by the name of Peter Becker. Becker confirmed in just a minute or two that Grammer was in fact there for his shift the night before. I thanked the man, ended the call, and dialed

Halloway. My phone rang in my ear. Three or four rings later, the captain picked up.

"Halloway," he answered.

"It's Harrington," I said. I let out a breath. "I want to get your take on something. I'm not really sure what we should do with this guy."

"Well, let me hear it. What do we have and not have?"

I ran through it with him. While we had information that said he wasn't responsible, we couldn't ignore the evidence that put him with the woman around the time of her death.

"I think you have to make the arrest," the captain said. "His prints on a dead woman. Admits to being with her in the general time in question."

"I don't think he's responsible," I said. "Call it a gut feeling combined with everything else. No violent priors. His vehicle doesn't match up with our witness account. He was at work during the shooting last night where we have another hand reported missing. Plus, he doesn't seem to be injured, and we think our shooter was. I think this guy just happened to pick up the wrong hooker at the wrong time."

"Can you prove that?" Halloway asked. "Anyone who can? Anyone who saw the woman alive after this guy finished his date with her?"

"He gave me a description of a woman who he says could. Another prostitute."

"Any way to find her?"

"Maybe. Let me try calling Vice. I'll let you know what's up here in a little bit."

"Okay."

"I left the scene with Steve if you need anything there," I said.

"I talked to him. He let the cameras know we were going to put together a real press conference later in the day. I wanted to try to get everyone together so we can get something drawn up for that prior to going on the record."

"All right. Let me get this shit taken care of here. One way or another," I said.

CHAPTER 16

A small bit of blood seeped from the dressed wound on Clifford's arm. He thought he'd done a pretty nice job on the sutures. Barring any kind of infection, he figured it would heal up without needing additional medical attention. Clifford took his eyes from his arm and looked at the television. The news he'd been watching had come back from commercials. The pair of anchors were droning on and on about some political nonsense. Clifford didn't have much interest in the topic and was trying to find something on the shooting. He flipped channels to the next local station, but some early morning game show was on. He continued surfing, finding more commercials on the following two local news channels.

Grumbling, he left the channel on. He leaned back farther in his recliner. The movement caused him to wince. His entire body hurt. Aside from the gunshot wound to his arm, each round that the body armor caught left him with a nasty bruise beneath. By his count, he'd been shot a total of seven times. The buckshot that hit him in the chest had left a ten-inch circular bruise. Clifford reached for the bottle of painkillers on the table next to his chair and emptied some into his hand. He washed them down with a couple of fingers of whiskey.

Clifford closed his eyes and tried to catch some sleep. As he lay there, his nose was filled with the smells wafting from the kitchen. The smell of the bubbling boiling pot cooking the flesh from the man's hand was almost appetizing. He took in a big breath, letting the smell fill every section of his airways. Minutes passed. The words "breaking news" and "Liberty City" yanked him from the verge of sleep.

He leaned forward in his chair and clicked the volume up. The reporter was on location, and a man in a suit stood before a bunch of patrol cars with their lights flashing. Beside the man was what looked like a detective in a suit. The man was reporting from the location where Clifford had been just hours before. The top of the screen said "Pre-recorded," as if Clifford couldn't make the connection that the footage was recorded at nighttime and it was now daylight. The reporter asked the cop, a Sergeant Chestnut from the Miami Homicide Bureau, what had happened. The cop didn't have a ton to say aside from the fact that there was a shooting with multiple casualties. He said they were just beginning their investigation and that if anyone was in the area and saw anything, they should call their local police department. The reporter asked if there were any leads. The cop stated that they had multiple witnesses and would have a press conference when they knew more. The pre-recorded footage ended a moment later, and the news coverage went back to the studio.

"Hmm," Clifford said. He grabbed his remote control for the television and did another lap through the local stations. He found another cop being interviewed. The background was similar to that of the other television footage—they were on location in Liberty City. Clifford immediately noticed that it was daylight. The footage couldn't have been more than an hour or two old. The cop who was speaking looked broad chested. He had a brown buzz cut. The ID at the bottom of the screen said his name was Sergeant Walsh, and the cop was again from Miami Homicide. This reporter seemed to know more than the reporter from the other channel and asked the cop if the shooter was a lone gunman. "As far as we know," the cop said. The reporter asked if the witness accounts were accurate when they stated the shooter was wearing body armor. The cop said they were checking into the statements regarding the man's description.

The reporter asked the cop if he could comment on the fact that it was an unprovoked attack. The cop seemed hesitant to answer. He said they were still trying to piece together what happened. He said the Miami-Dade PD planned a press conference later in the day and would have more details then. Like the cop interviewed earlier, he asked for the public's help. If they had seen any vehicle or person on foot leaving the area the prior night, they were asked to please come forward. Clifford couldn't help noticing that neither of the two cops had mentioned anything about the missing hands. They had to have known.

He figured they'd found the hooker—and the discovery of both a hooker and a man with chopped-off hands inside of a couple of days probably wouldn't be chalked up to coincidence. Perhaps it was information that they wanted to keep out of the press. Clifford didn't care what their reasoning was. He had no interest in public recognition for what he was doing. All he required was the thrill of a successful hunt and the proof of his personal conquest in the form of his trophies.

The reporting turned from on-location footage back to the studio. The television anchors spoke of how the police would be patrolling the area. They said police would have an increased presence on the streets until this person was found and brought to justice. The mention of the police and their patrols sparked a thought in Clifford's head. He had an idea. A smile overtook his face.

CHAPTER 17

Henry Grammer was placed under arrest and transferred to our holding facility. The admission that he was with the woman—and fingerprint evidence—was too much for us not to place him in custody. And with him in custody, we had a couple of days to work and hopefully get a better picture of his involvement without having to worry that he was responsible and left out on the street.

I'd already made the call to Vice to ask if they knew of a prostitute who matched Grammer's description. Tillerson said that the description didn't ring a bell off the top of his head, but he'd call around and see if it struck a chord with anyone else. He said he'd spread the word on the woman and let his people know to pick her up if they spotted her.

Dealing with Grammer, the arrest, and getting him picked up took a few hours. During that time, Steve called and let me know they were wrapping up on scene. He'd also said that he got ambushed by the press and gave them a generic sound bite on the case—we'd just begun the investigation, we would like the public's help, and we'd give them more at a later date.

Halloway gave my office door a knock and walked in. "When did you get back?"

"About an hour ago," I said.

He took a seat across from me at my desk. "I must have just missed you when I left. The missus and I went to lunch. Anniversary," he said.

"Today?" I asked.

"Twenty-three years today," he said.

"Congrats," I said.

"It's been all right," Halloway said. "Can't complain too much. No one would listen if I did. So, we have Mr. Grammer locked up and an unknown shooter, responsible for at least five deaths, on the loose. The unknown shooter could possibly be the person responsible for what we currently have Grammer locked up for."

"That's the gist of it," I said.

"And the hand, or I guess I should say the lack thereof, is the only thing that connects the two occurrences."

"Correct," I said. "Pretty damn good connection, though. It's not like chopped-off hands are commonplace."

"Did we get anything else from the two people that were shot and at the hospital?"

"I just talked to Garcia a couple minutes ago. He interviewed both. A man and a woman. Neither gave him more than what we already had on our shooter."

"Which was?"

"Basically nothing. A guy in black tactical gear and body armor. With some kind of mask. Rough height and weight, which could best be described as average. No race, no identifiable features, no hair color, no nothing. No vehicle as well. Shit, we don't even know if it was a male. After Monica Hyland's little revenge-seeking murder spree, I'm not ruling a woman out of anything." Our female killer from a recent case was still fresh on my mind.

I continued, "At least if someone had witnessed a truck similar to the one seen with Kylie Bowe, we would have been able to make a connection. We thought we were going to get somewhere with a camera mounted on a house up the block. Turns out, the camera was a fake. It was an empty housing with an LED light run by batteries. Steve contacted the guy whose house it was on. A deterrent, the guy called it."

"Useless, more like," the captain said.

"Exactly. So, we have not much of anything unless Colt or Skip can come up with something. All we really have to work with there are whatever rounds were pulled from the scene and bodies."

"What about shell casings?" Halloway asked.

"Tons of them. I think Colt said that he picked up forty-one forty-five caliber casings that we attribute to our unknown shooter. Not a print or partial on a single one of them."

"Loaded while wearing gloves."

"I guess," I said.

"What are you and the guys on now?" the captain asked.

"Garcia isn't back from interviewing the pair that were shot yet. I'll probably go have him rattle Colt's cage for an update when he returns. As far as Steve and Ryan, I sent them over to lock up to have a quick chat with Michelle

Dirol and Leon 'Coolie' Reese. I wanted to see if either knew who this red-haired woman was."

The captain furrowed his brows. "Red-haired woman?"

"Remember when I said that Grammer told me he chatted another hooker up after he dropped Kylie Bowe off? Someone who could potentially verify his story?"

"Yeah. This red-haired woman was her?"

"Correct. I got word from Vice earlier that they'd look for her tonight, but we don't have a ton of leads to hunt down at the moment. Maybe if we can find this woman, she can corroborate Grammer's story. More importantly, if Grammer's story is true, there's a chance that this woman may have actually seen who Kylie Bowe last left with."

"Okay. That's something at least. When do you think you can sit down with Mark and me?"

Mark, I assumed, was Mark Swanson from the PD's PR department. "For the press release?" I asked.

"Yeah, I'd like to have something together for the evening news. They've been reporting on the shooting all day. You couldn't miss the coverage if you tried. They keep replaying the footage of Chestnut and Walsh, saying we don't know anything, over and over."

"We really don't. Not much has changed there," I said.

"We should give them something official."

I shrugged. "All I'm doing now is searching the internet for anything regarding missing hands, as in, cut off. I found a couple cases that were from some years back in Tampa. A couple of cases across the US. Nothing really seems similar."

"Maybe try calling Agent Couch over at the bureau," the

captain said. "He may be able to come up with something."

"Probably not the worst idea," I said.

Most cops were leery about asking the FBI for assistance. The idea that the bureau automatically swooped in and took over every case they heard about was ingrained in a lot of people who worked law enforcement—the public as well for that matter. I figured television had something to do with it. But they were a hell of a resource to have and had their own cases and workload to worry about. Unless it was something huge and out of our scope, or we specifically asked them to come in on a case, there was about a zero percent chance that they'd forcefully take over one of our active investigations. On top of that, I'd worked closely with Agent Couch, who led the special investigations department at the Miramar FBI field office, a number of times. He'd never been anything but forthright.

"You do that," the captain said. "I'll go round up Mark. Let's say twenty minutes in my office."

"I'll be over," I said.

The captain rose from his chair and left my office. I looked up Couch's number in my contacts and dialed him from my desk.

"Couch," he answered.

"Hey, Couch. It's Harrington over at Miami Homicide."

"Lieutenant, how are you doing?" he asked.

"Not too bad. Yourself?" I asked.

"Ah. I'm still kicking. That's something."

"It is."

"Well, what's up? I imagine something? Probably having

something to do with a shootout in Liberty City would be my guess."

"That it would," I said. "Been watching television?"

"Hard to miss the coverage," he said. "And whoever went in there shooting is pretty damn brazen. So, what can we do? What do you need?"

"Well, first, I have a little more information for you that isn't in the coverage."

"I'm listening," Couch said.

"One of the victims of the shooting had their hand removed."

"Removed?"

"With a hatchet," I said. "And we had a dead prostitute the evening before. She shows a similar wound. One of her hands missing as well."

"Hmm. Shot?" he asked. "The prostitute?"

"Strangled and beaten," I said.

"But everyone shot on the scene in Liberty City?"

"Yeah," I said. "We have a witness report of a large dark-colored SUV in the area where we found the prostitute. No such report of a vehicle on the Liberty City scene. Also, we have someone in custody in connection with the prostitute, but he has a verified alibi when it comes to the shootout last night."

"Hands missing from both, but you can only tie the guy that you're holding to one?"

"Yeah."

"What's linking him to the woman?"

"Prints on her and his admission that he was with her in our window of TOD."

"Hmm," Couch said. "I don't know what to make of what you have going on there. Gang initiation of some sort? How old is the guy that you have in custody?"

"Fifties."

"Damn, it would have been a halfway plausible theory had the age checked out. I doubt a fifty-some-year-old is out killing and chopping off hands to show loyalty to a gang. What's your gut tell you on the guy you're holding?"

"Unless he has an accomplice that did the Liberty City thing, he isn't our guy," I said. "There are a couple other things that don't line up as well, but—"

"But you can't just dismiss the evidence that you have," he said.

"Right."

"Well, what can I do to help?"

"Maybe see if anyone has seen something like this before. If any of your guys have heard of someone taking people's hands."

"You know. I had a question on the tip of my tongue before and was going to ask, but we got off the subject."

"Shoot," I said.

"On this shootout, only one hand was taken, correct?"

"Yeah. Just one person's hand removed."

"Maybe check into that guy's history. See if you can tie him to the prostitute," Couch said.

I nodded as he said it. "Yeah. That's not the worst idea. I'll put one of my guys on it."

"I'll make some calls and see what, if anything, I can find out. Maybe I'll try giving Agent Rawlings in Manassas a ring and see if the homicide division of the special investigations has anything in their system."

"I'd appreciate whatever help you can lend."

"Okay. Give me a couple hours and let me see if I can find anything out. I'll give you a ring around six."

"Perfect," I said.

"Talk soon."

Couch clicked off, and I tossed my phone on its base. I rocked back in my chair in thought. Hopefully Couch could find us something. We were slim on leads, and the longer things remained that way, the more the public would be stirred into a frenzy.

CHAPTER 18

The press release we put out was fairly short and sweet. Mark managed to spin the fact that we didn't have anything and had just started our investigation into something press worthy. Kylie Bowe wasn't mentioned. The connection of the missing hands wasn't mentioned. Until we knew more, we felt it was best to keep a lid on that information. The captain thought the hand removal might be the way of a killer seeking recognition for his crimes. The media were told that we'd report again as more information came in.

I got the time from my watch—a quarter after six. My team had all left. Steve and Ryan hadn't gotten a thing from talking to Michelle Dirol or Leon Reese—neither had admitted that they'd ever seen a red-haired woman in the area where Kylie Bowe had worked. Either they were lying about having never seen the woman, which was certainly possible, or the woman herself didn't exist, which was another possibility. Time would tell.

I hadn't heard anything back from Couch over at the FBI. I figured I'd give him a buzz before taking off. On the chance that he forgot he was going to call, or something came up on his end, I didn't want to waste my evening waiting for a call that might never come. I dialed his office and held my phone to my ear with my shoulder. His phone rang a few times before his voicemail picked up. I left him a message that I was headed home for the day and gave him my cell number to call if he'd come up with anything. I tossed my phone on its base, shut down my computer, and grabbed my keys from my desk. I'd put in my almost thirteen hours for the day.

I killed the lights in my office and closed the door. The moment I did, I heard my phone ring inside. Couch calling, I figured.

I pushed the door open, flicked my office lights on, and picked up the ringing phone.

"Harrington," I answered.

"Hey. It's Tillerson. We have your girl."

"The redhead?"

"Yeah. I made a couple of calls. Some of the guys out working spotted her and scooped her up. Where do you want her?"

"Here, I guess," I said.

"Okay. Call it twenty minutes or so and I'll have them bring her by."

"Sure. What's her name?"

"Charlotte Burrell. Listed address is Newnan, Georgia. Not sure where she resides here in Florida, but she'd been popped for soliciting in the area twice over the last year, so she's been here for a bit."

"Okay," I said.

"Do you want her brought into the front?"

"Yeah, I'll be down there waiting."

"Sounds good. I'll let them know. Anything else?" he asked.

"Nope. Thanks, Tillerson. We owe you one."

"You got it," he said.

I clicked off from the call and powered up my computer. After it booted, I ran the woman's name in search of her sheet. She came up right away. The woman was thirty-one. She was five foot eleven, and in her state-issued identification, she had thin-looking, almost white blond hair. Her eyes looked sunken, and her cheekbones protruded from her face. The photo made her appear sickly. Drugs, I imagined. I scrolled to the priors. Tillerson was right. She had been busted for soliciting in the area two times over the last year or so. She'd also been busted another three times in Georgia a couple of years before for the same reason. A few possession charges and other random offenses were sprinkled in as well.

My cell phone buzzed in my pocket. I slid it out and looked at the caller's number, which was blocked. I clicked Talk.

"Lieutenant Harrington," I answered.

"Hey, it's Couch. Sorry it took me a bit to get back to you. It's been a little busy around here."

"No problem," I said.

"I wish I had something good to tell you, but the truth is I don't really have anything at all."

"All right," I said.

"We don't have anything in any of our databases about a

guy cutting off single hands and taking them from scenes. With this guy, if it's the same guy, choosing to strangle one and shoot others, we can't really connect any dots on a signature there, either. I called up to Manassas and got Agent Rawlings on the phone. I guess he went through their system up there as well. Nothing, unfortunately."

"Okay. Well, it was worth a shot," I said.

"One thing we could still try is running the ballistics information through our databases, though," Couch said. "Maybe we can get a hit."

"Sure. I think our crime lab guys are still working on it, but I'll put them into contact with you and we can see what shakes out."

"Works for me," Couch said. "Just have them call me when it's set."

"Will do. I appreciate the help, as always," I said.

"No problem."

I clicked off from the call and sent a quick text message to Colt to forward the ballistics information on to Couch at the bureau. Through the open blinds of the front glass of my office, I could see the empty desks of my team in the bull pen. I looked past them at Halloway's office. He was still in. I called him at his desk and gave him a quick update on what was going on. Halloway told me to call him when I had the woman in an interview room.

I left my office and headed downstairs. In the front lobby, I waited with a view outside at the turnaround in front of the building. While I waited, I called the Midwest station out front and let them know that I'd be bringing a woman in and would need to use one of their interview rooms. I was told they were both empty and it wouldn't be a problem.

Ten minutes passed before a silver Chevy sedan pulled up. The car wasn't marked. Both front doors opened, and two guys in street clothes exited. A woman was in the back of the car, yet I couldn't make out if she was our woman in question or not. One of the men, the driver, had longer hair pulled into a ponytail. The passenger was bald and wearing a Hawaiian shirt with a shoulder-holstered firearm. The driver rounded the front of his car, and a lanyard with a badge was hanging from his neck. The man was also carrying.

I started walking toward the front doors of the building while watching the guys through the glass. The pair started up the sidewalk for our building's entrance. I went outside to meet them.

"Lieutenant Harrington," I said. The guys were about twenty feet away, still approaching. "Tillerson said you'd be bringing her."

"Street corner to front door service," the man who'd been driving said. "Detective Nathan Frost." He held out his hand for a handshake, which I took. Frost looked the better part of forty-five. His skin was weathered, and most of his cheeks and chin hid under an inch or so of graying-brown beard. Aside from his service weapon and badge, he wore black jeans and a black motorcycle T-shirt. I'd seen the guy around before. Where, I couldn't put my finger on. Some police function in the past, I imagined. The undercover guys tried to limit their mingling with the regular force, for good reason. "This is Detective David Nance," Frost said.

I shook the bald detective's hand. I didn't recognize him, but even with the Hawaiian shirt that was unbuttoned one too many buttons, and the gold chains, watch, and bracelets, there was something about him that screamed cop—he might as well have been wearing a uniform.

"Where did you find her?" I asked.

"A few blocks from Seventy-Ninth in the neighborhood in question," Detective Frost said. "She's fairly regular around there. Tillerson put the word out to keep eyes open for the woman. We took a ride over to the neighborhood where she usually works, and there she was, leaning into someone's car. About as easy as it gets."

"I appreciate you picking her up. Are you dropping her here or what?" I asked.

The bald one, Detective Nance, shook his head. "We picked her up in the act of soliciting. She's under arrest. After you're through with her here, we'll take her in."

"Fair enough," I said. "I'm going to take her into the patrol building there." I pointed at the building. "Did you guys want to come in and wait?"

The two looked at each other.

"How long are you thinking?" Frost asked.

"Half hour. Maybe less."

"Tillerson didn't really get into why we were bringing her over here," Frost said. "What's up with her?"

I gave the guys a brief overview of the investigation. "I'm basically trying to get a confirmation on an alibi from her," I said. "Poke around a little bit and see if she knows anything else."

"All right. We'll probably just hang out outside here. Park the car and catch up on some paperwork."

"Not a problem," I said.

The guys pulled the woman from the back of the car and passed her over to me along with a key to the woman's cuffs. As Grammer had described, her hair was about the brightest red imaginable, and as in the photo on her driver's license, she looked sickly. Her cheeks were sunken. Her eyes were glazed. She stank of marijuana and alcohol. I pointed the detectives to where they should park and took the woman into the patrol building.

At the front desk, we were buzzed through, and I escorted Charlotte Burrell down the hall toward the interview rooms. She hadn't said a single word since she'd been taken from the car.

In interview room one, I unhooked the cuffs from behind her back and sat her at the metal table.

"Ms. Burrell, I'm Lieutenant Harrington with Miami Homicide."

She didn't respond but simply stared at her feet. Enclosed in the room with her, I noticed that the smell of weed and booze coming off her had intensified.

"I need to ask you some questions about the other night."

"What night?" she asked. Her voice was a bit slurred.

I let out a big breath. I wasn't entirely certain that she was in a state of mind to be helpful.

"Sunday into Monday morning," I said.

"What about it?" she asked.

"Do you know a woman named Kylie Bowe?" I asked.

"Woman?" she asked. "I know a girl named Kylie. Can't be much more than twenty, the one I know."

"She's in the same line of work and does that in the same area as you?"

"I don't know what you're talking about," she said.

"Weren't you picked up for soliciting?" I asked. "And we have your sheet with your priors."

"I was talking to a friend. I was doing nothing wrong."

"Sure," I said. "I actually don't care one way or another what you were doing. I just need you to answer some questions about Kylie Bowe. Now, do you remember her being around Sunday night and early Monday morning?"

"I don't know. Maybe. Why are you asking me questions about her?" Ms. Burrell looked up. "What happened to her?"

"She was killed," I said.

"Killed?"

"Yes," I said.

"Does Coolie know?" she asked.

"Is he a friend of yours?"

"Acquaintance," she said.

"He's aware. He's also in custody."

"He didn't do it," she said.

"That's not what he's in custody for. He had warrants. Now, do you remember seeing her?"

"Maybe," she said.

"What about you talking to a man in a dark sedan who dropped her off?" I asked.

"I don't remember talking to anyone," she said.

"You don't remember talking to a guy who dropped her

off and asking him if he could go another round or something to that effect? And him responding with a joke that he wasn't as young as he once was?"

She nodded. "Yeah. I remember that now that you bring it up. He did drop her off, but I didn't solicit him."

"Whatever," I said. "You talked to him?"

"A little," she said.

"Do you think you'd recognize the guy if you saw him?" I asked.

"I don't know. Maybe."

"Did he say he'd look for you the next time he was in the area?"

"He may have said something to that effect."

It fit with what he'd said and was probably the closest to a yes that I was going to get out of her.

"Do you remember what happened after that?"

"What do you mean?" she asked.

"If Kylie Bowe got into another vehicle," I said.

"The last I saw her, she was hopping into the passenger side of a big SUV that I thought was a cop."

"Why did you think it was a cop?" I asked.

"I'm not stupid. I take in my surroundings. That truck had been parked in the grocery store lot for an hour or more and then crossed the street to try to get a date. What would someone be over there watching for if they weren't a cop?"

"They could be watching to make sure that one of you weren't a cop."

"Do I look like a cop to you?" she asked.

"So, a big dark SUV," I said. It was the second time that

we'd heard that description of the vehicle. "Anything else to add to that?"

"It was different looking. Like it should be in the jungle or on a safari or something."

"What specifically was making it look like that?" I asked.

"It was tall. Big tires. There was a basket on top and a bunch of other things stuck to it," she said.

"Do you think if we showed you some photos of different trucks or SUVs that you could pick it out?" I asked.

"Maybe."

"Hang tight for me. I'll be back with you in just a second."

She nodded.

I rose from my chair and left the office. I needed to get a picture of Grammer and some photos of different vehicles printed up and put in front of her.

CHAPTER 19

Clifford's plan was straightforward. He needed two things—the cover of darkness and a license plate. The time to get the plate had come. Clifford pulled the license plate off his rental vehicle and drove to a high-traffic retail area about ten minutes from his house. The mall in the center of everything held hundreds of stores. Beyond the parking lot of the mall were countless outbuildings and restaurants.

He drove up and down aisle after aisle until he found one with a few cars backed in. He backed his rental car into a free spot in the aisle of parked cars and killed the motor. He stepped out and looked over the roof of his car toward the mall. While countless people were coming and going from the nearest mall entrance and exits, no one came down his aisle. Clifford walked to the back of his car and had a look around again. He saw a woman getting into a car five or six down. He pulled the screwdriver from his pocket and went to the back of the first car that had backed in—a couple-year-old Honda econobox. Clifford pulled the plate off and set it on the ground behind the car before moving to the next backed-in vehicle.

Looking around, he stayed low. He saw no one. The plate for the second vehicle, a full-size Ford sedan, was next to come off. Clifford took the Ford's plate to the Honda and screwed it on. He took the Honda's plate to his car and secured it to the back. While the stolen plate had a good chance of being reported, his thinking was that the Honda owner wouldn't notice their plate was different. At least that was what Clifford hoped. He needed the plate only for the night, so he figured his chances were good.

Clifford took his seat behind the wheel and pulled from the parking spot.

CHAPTER 20

The printer kicked out the final photo that I'd printed. I placed it with the others in a file and left the back office of the Midwest Patrol building. My phone buzzed in my pocket as I walked. I pulled it out and had a quick look at the screen—a text from Amy. She was inquiring about when I'd be done and what my current thoughts on dinner were. I'd have to text her back when I was finished with Ms. Burrell, who was still waiting in the interview room where I left her. I pulled the door open and walked to my chair.

"Do you know how long I'm going to be here?" she asked.

"Are you in a rush to get booked?"

She put her hand into her bright red hair and fluffed it. "The sooner I get in, the sooner I'll get out. Unless you're going to get me a deal for helping you?"

"I'll tell you what. I'm going to show you some photos of vehicles, and I want you to tell me if any of them match up with the vehicle you last saw her get into. You help me out with that and give me a written statement of your interaction with the guy who dropped Kylie Bowe off, and I'll talk to the two detectives who picked you up and see if maybe they can do something about not taking you in. Now that's not me saying you'll get off. That's me saying that I'll talk to them."

"Fine," she said.

"First, though, I want you to look at a different photo. Was this the guy that you talked to the other night? The one who dropped Kylie Bowe off and made the joke?" I opened the folder and slid a copy of Grammer's DL photo toward her.

She shrugged. "I want to say yes, but I can't be one hundred percent."

I kind of figured that was going to be her response, considering it was nighttime and he had been inside a car. I'd printed a photo of his make and model of vehicle as well. "What about this? Was this the car that the guy was driving when he dropped her off?"

She looked at the photo for a second. "Yeah, that looks like it."

"All right," I said.

I placed a statement sheet in front of her and had her fill it out with her account of the night in question. A couple of minutes passed while she worked on her statement, and I got all my photos of SUVs in order.

"That's it," she said. Ms. Burrell slid her completed statement toward me.

I took a second to read through it. It was what she'd told me to the letter. I set the statement, the photo of Grammer's DL picture, and the photo of his vehicle to the side and scooped up the file with the photos of SUVs in it. "These are the SUVs I want you to have a look at for me."

She nodded but said nothing.

I opened the folder, pulled out the top picture, and slid it across the metal desk toward her. The print was of a lifted four-door Jeep.

She shook her head and pushed it toward me. "Close, but no. This thing was longer, bigger, and I don't know, more plain looking. It wasn't a Jeep. It had a top. Then it had a rack on top of it, or basket or whatever they're called. Something on its roof for carrying things."

I pulled the photo toward me and turned it facedown on the table.

"Did the vehicle look new or old?" I asked.

"I couldn't say," she said.

I pulled out a photo of a 1990s Land Cruiser from the file and passed it to her. She looked at it for a moment and passed it back.

"It was squarer than that," she said.

I rummaged through the file and found a photo of a previous generation Land Cruiser that was, in fact, squarer.

She squinted as she held the picture. Her face looked torn. "It's close," she said. "It was boxy like that. About the same length, but I guess it was probably newer than whatever this is."

I spread the other photos out and looked for something closer. I pulled a photo of a newer 4Runner out and showed it to her. She responded that the car she'd seen wasn't that new looking in the front.

"It kind of looked like a military vehicle," she said.

I found a photo of a Humvee. "Like this?"

"No. That's too military looking. This wasn't as wide as that, either."

I let out a long breath and took every photo of an SUV that I'd printed out and set them on the table side by side in front of her. I watched her eyes go from one picture to the next.

"I want to say that it kind of looks like this, but I'm still not a hundred percent," she said. I looked at the photo that she pointed at, which was of a Mercedes SUV. The truck was normally referred to as a G wagon or G-Class.

"But still not it?" I asked. "What is different, exactly?"

"What she climbed into was bigger."

"Like taller?" I asked.

"Yeah, but just a bigger vehicle in general. Can you just try searching for a safari truck or something like that on your phone and see what comes up? I really think that was what it was. I bet we can find it that way."

I didn't have a clue what she considered a safari truck or what a safari truck's traits were in her mind, but I took out my phone and typed in the info. I scrolled the page, having a quick look, then simply sat next to her so she could see the screen. I continued scrolling.

"Stop!" she said. "Go back up. That was it."

I scrolled up the page a couple of vehicles.

"That one there," she said.

Center on my cell phone's screen was a four-door Land Rover Defender.

"Yeah. That's it," she said.

I knew a little about the truck, mostly that every European bad guy in movies had an entourage that drove them. Yet I couldn't remember ever seeing one in real life. I punched the name of the truck's maker into my phone and found that most every photo was of a right-hand drive vehicle. In another minute or two of searching, I learned that the vehicle had been sold in the United States in only one year—1993. I'd also learned that anyone who owned that vehicle now owned something worth about the price of a house. Aside from the truck information, I got another text from Amy asking if I wanted to do dinner and a movie. She again asked when I'd be home. I fired off a quick response consisting of the words *sure* and *half hour*. I went back to the truck information on my phone.

"Was the driver on the right side?" I asked. I looked up at Ms. Burrell, who had taken to picking at her teeth with her long fake fingernail in a color that matched her hair.

"What?" she asked.

"The driver. Was the steering wheel on the normal side of the guy's truck or on the other side like a mail truck?"

She took her fingernail from her mouth and clasped her hands in front of herself. "I'm pretty sure Kylie got in the passenger side. I mean, nothing seemed odd about her getting into the guy's truck."

"Okay," I said. "Let me just get the fact that you identified this truck added to your statement and then we'll get you out of here."

"And you'll go talk to the two undercover guys that

picked me up and tell them to let me go."

"And then I'll go talk to them," I said. "No promises."

"Yeah," she said.

I added to her statement the fact that she visually identified a truck, then I listed the make and model and had her initial it. When she finished, I asked her to sit tight while I went and found the detectives who had brought her. Detectives Frost and Nance had said they were going to wait in their car and catch up on some paperwork. I'd pointed them to some visitor parking off the side of the main entrance. As I walked from the front of the building, I could see their car parked there. Detective Frost stood outside the driver's door. He leaned against the fender facing me and smoked a cigarette. I got within fifty feet when he saw me walking toward him.

"All set?" he asked.

"I'm done with her. I just wanted to have one of you come in and get her," I said.

"Sure," Frost said. He took a big drag of his smoke. "Did you get what you needed?" he asked, exhaling.

"She was actually pretty helpful," I said.

The passenger door opened, and Detective Nance stepped from the car. "Let's get her and get out of here. I'd like to get home before tomorrow," he said.

"What are the chances of her getting kicked loose for helping me out?" I asked.

"We caught her in the act," Frost said. "How valuable was her information?"

"Pretty damn valuable," I said. "Maybe freed someone

who wasn't guilty and got us closer to catching up with someone who is."

"I don't care one way or another. Whether we take her in or not, she's going to go back out on the corner the second she can," Nance said.

"Do you want us to kick her loose?" Frost asked. He took another puff of his smoke.

"I'm leaving it up to you," I said. "She helped, but like you said, she's probably going to go back to doing exactly what she was doing. If I picked her up, I'd probably send her on her way with some kind of warning along the lines of someone from her corner was murdered and she won't have information to offer next time. Maybe that mixed with a 'We'll be watching for you.'"

"All right," Frost said. "Let's go that route." He put his cigarette out on the ground and tossed the butt into a garbage can a few feet from the front of their parked car.

"Let's get her from inside," Nance said.

I led the way into the building.

CHAPTER 21

I thanked the detectives and watched them drive away with Charlotte Burrell in the back of their car. While they were in the interview room, they'd informed her that they were going to let her loose where they found her and gave her a warning. I added a bit about her maybe choosing a new profession, which I was fairly certain she would ignore or dismiss. In any case, she thanked me for talking to the detectives.

After talking with the guys in Patrol and getting a BOLO on the vehicle, I'd walked back into the homicide bureau and into my office to go through the process of shutting down again—my computer was powered down, the lights turned off, the door locked. If it had been normal office hours, I would have been making phone calls to see what I could do about getting Grammer out of his holding cell. That late, however, nothing could be done until morning. He'd be spending the night in lockup, and while it was unfortunate, if he hadn't picked up a prostitute in the first place, he could have avoided the entire situation.

I popped into Dave's office on my way out, told him about Burrell and the truck, and brought him up to speed as fast as I could. He said he'd call me with any updates overnight. I let out a big breath as I used my foot to open the station's back door to the parking lot. My Bronco sat by itself fifty yards away. I pulled out my phone as I walked, seeing another pair of text messages from Amy letting me know that a half hour had passed. I dialed her.

"You're late," she said and laughed.

"Sorry. You know how it is," I said. "I'm just walking out, though. What's up?"

"Nothing. Waiting on you."

"Dinner and a movie?" I asked.

"Yeah, that's fine. I just want to get out and do something," she said.

Although I was beat and didn't really want to do much more than lie on the couch and fall asleep, I felt as though I owed her something for making her wait on me to get off work.

"Whatever you want to do, babe." I pulled the door handle for my truck and jumped inside. "I'm just leaving. Be home in a couple minutes."

"Sounds good," she said. "Love you, bye."

"Love you, bye," I said.

I clicked off from the call and jammed my phone into my pocket. I stuck the key into the truck's ignition and turned it. I got a single click.

"Come on," I said.

I tried again. Nothing. Not even a click.

"Don't be a bitch, Lucille," I said. I turned the key again to the sound of silence. "I just asked you to not be a bitch."

I pulled the key from the ignition and reached across the

truck for the glove box, where I grabbed my headlamp. I'd been stranded in the truck at night before and had all the necessary equipment to fix or at least assess the situation. I strapped on the light, clicked it on, and hopped out of my truck. My plan was simple. I was going to grab the biggest wrench from the box in the back, slide under my truck, and whack the daylights out of the starter. As a kid growing up, I'd seen my father use the "fix" a couple of times. I needed it to work only once. I tossed a moving company blanket from the back of my truck on the ground beside my driver's door and slid my way underneath. With eyes on the starter, I gave it a couple of good smacks with the back end of a half-inch drive ratchet. I scooted out, opened the driver's door, and stuck the key in the ignition.

"Come on," I said. I turned the key. Nothing.

I mumbled a few profanities and quickly went through my options. Doing anything other than letting the truck sit and grabbing a cruiser from the lot ended with me covered in grease—and with an annoyed girlfriend. Swapping the starter was a pretty quick job, but it could wait until the morning. I walked to the office, where I could get a set of keys. After a quick shit shooting with Oscar Borges, the sixty-year-old officer who worked the booth where we signed out keys for the cruisers, I was on my way.

I pulled the unmarked gray Crown Vic into my driveway and walked into the house. Lucky did her best to maul me with excitement. I crouched, gave her a good petting, then moved slowly past the front doorway, yawning into my fist as I looked around for Amy. The television was on and played the music channel, yet I didn't see Amy in the living room. The lights in the kitchen were off. The lights on the back patio and bar area were off. A second later, I heard the click-clack of shoes coming down the hallway that led to our bedroom. Amy appeared a moment later. She wore a black dress that was far too fancy for anything resembling dinner and a movie.

"What's with the fanciness?" I asked.

"I thought maybe we could skip the movie and just go to The Grill. We should get there with plenty of time to eat but not early enough where we'd need a reservation."

The Grill was a trendy chophouse in downtown Miami. We'd been there a few times in the past, and from experience, I knew that it was almost impossible not to drop a few hundred dollars by walking into the place. I thought about it a bit further. While I could probably fall asleep at any moment, I needed to eat, and the steaks at the place were pretty damn good. I scratched at the stubble on my cheek. It had been awhile since we'd gone out someplace nice.

"Sure," I said. "What the hell. Let me change."

Amy was working an earring into her ear. She walked to me, wrapped her arms around my neck, and gave me a kiss. "We should be good if we leave in a half hour or so."

"Okay. Let me shower quick, change, and we'll take off. You have to drive, though. Or at least we have to take your car. The Bronco is broken. I had to take a cruiser from the lot."

"This is me looking surprised," Amy said.

Her face was stoic. She didn't look surprised.

"It's minor," I said.

"What's wrong with it?" she asked.

"Starter."

"I thought you got a new one a week or two ago," she said.

"I did. I just didn't get a chance to put it in."

"Is that something that takes a long time to do?"

I shook my head. "Not at all if everything goes as it should. Disconnect the battery. Take the wire from the starter solenoid. Slide under the truck, two bolts, pull the starter out, and stick the new one in."

"Why don't we just go fix it?" she asked.

I furrowed my brows. "We?"

"Sure. I'll hand you wrenches and be there for moral support." Amy dropped her arms from my neck and sat on the edge of our recliner.

"You're already all dressed up," I said. "And looking good, by the way."

Amy smiled. "Thanks, and it'll take two seconds for me to throw on some jeans and a sweatshirt."

"What about eating, though?" I stuck a finger in my neckline and loosened my tie.

"I'll make us a couple sandwiches," she said. "You go change."

"Are you sure? Babe, I can just swap it out in the morning and we can go get steaks."

"Positive. It'll be fun. I'll throw down a blanket, bring a bottle of wine, and it'll be like a late-night picnic under the stars."

"You mean under the light poles of a police station parking lot," I said. "Plus, I think they call that drinking in public."

"It sounds romantic to me," she said. "And if the cops come, I'll stash the hooch."

I laughed. "All right. I'm sold."

CHAPTER 22

"Come on," Clifford said. He stared into his rearview mirror. He didn't see the light bar of the patrol car behind him light up. He rubbed his eyes. "Unbelievable," he said. He swerved again.

Clifford had been driving around all night, actively trying to get a cop to pull him over. He'd racked up close to two hundred miles. The task of getting stopped by the police seemed exceptionally hard when one was looking for it. Around one in the morning, he sped past a patrol car in Hialeah. He did a good twenty miles an hour over the speed limit as he passed the cop then veered into the cop's lane. The cop did nothing and turned off on the next street.

Hours later, he spotted the next cop by luck as he was stopped at a red light. Clifford happened to look to his right and saw a patrol car parked in a North Miami gas station parking lot. The lights inside the car were on. Clifford could see the cop behind the wheel. He floored the gas, squealing the tires of his rental car and running the red light. Clifford slowed as he got to the other side of the intersection, waiting on the cop. The cop never came.

The cop who currently followed him had been on his tail for the better part of a mile. It was a few minutes after four in the morning. Clifford had been swerving all over the road, but the cop wasn't pulling him over for some reason. Clifford was certain the cop was following him. He'd made multiple lefts and rights, which the patrol car mirrored. Yet if the cop had run the plates, he would have seen that they didn't come back to the Chevy that Clifford drove.

He headed north on Spartan Boulevard. A college took up everything on the west side of the street. The homes on the east side all had large lots and were set back off the road. He didn't know if he would find a more suitable location for what he wanted to do. Clifford swerved violently again, putting two tires off the right side of the road into the grass shoulder. The cop's lights finally lit. Clifford continued up the block until he found quite possibly the perfect spot. A big empty lot with thick trees and vegetation sat just beyond the sidewalk to his right. Across the street to his left was one of the college's gated entrances. The gates were closed.

The patrol car's spotlight lit and blasted him in the face, reflecting from his driver's door mirror. A moment later, Clifford saw a break in the light as the officer approached his car.

"Do you have your license, registration, and proof of insurance?" the officer asked as he came to the window.

Clifford glanced up at the cop, who held a flashlight pointed at him. He squinted from the light. "No," he said. "I forgot my wallet." He caught the name on the pin affixed to the cop's shirt—Pazanis.

"Do you normally carry your vehicle registration in your wallet?" the officer asked.

"Um," Clifford said.

"What's your name?"

"I haven't been drinking," Clifford said.

"Step out of the car for me, sir," the officer said. He opened Clifford's door. "Please keep your hands where I can see them."

Clifford put one foot out then the other. He kept his hands open and visible. The lights from an approaching car grew nearer. Clifford wouldn't stand until the car passed. As the other vehicle went by, he looked down in an attempt to obscure his face, which was lit by the cop's flashlight.

"Stand up, sir," the officer said. "Follow me to the back of the vehicle."

Clifford stood. He followed the cop's instructions and walked toward the rear of his rental car. The cop walked backward. Clifford got a good look at him behind his flashlight. The guy was bigger—an inch or two over six foot and a good fifty pounds overweight. He'd be a challenge to best, hand to hand.

"Do you know why I stopped you?"

"Because I was swerving all over the road," Clifford said. "That or the plates don't come back to this car. One of those two is my guess."

The cop looked at him with a question on his face.

Clifford looked past the cop and down the street. No cars approached. He glanced over his shoulder and saw no cars coming from that direction.

"Right now, you have the advantage," Clifford said. He turned toward the cop and locked eyes on him. Clifford reached to his back waistline. "It's kill or be killed. Survival of the fittest."

"Hands where I can see them," the officer said.

Clifford grasped the handle of his pistol. "I assume we're both wearing vests. Take that into consideration."

"Sir!" the officer said. The cop popped the thumb break on his hip holster.

Clifford was already lifting his gun before the cop could draw. He fired twice into the cop's legs. One shot to the cop's right kneecap was flawless. The officer's legs went out, and he dropped to the ground. The cop tried lifting his weapon to get a shot, but Clifford was on him in an instant. He kicked the cop's gun out of his hand, booted the officer in the face, and dragged him by his pant legs behind his patrol car. The cop screamed as he was being dragged. Clifford caught the cop going for his shoulder radio. He dropped the officer's legs to the ground, which caused him to scream louder. Clifford snatched the radio from the cop's shoulder and threw it into the brush in the empty lot.

Clifford mounted the cop's chest, putting a knee on each of his arms. He grasped his pistol by the barrel and brought the grip down into the cop's forehead. The blow opened a huge gash over the man's left eyebrow. Clifford raised his hand and slammed his weapon down again. He lifted again and struck again, repeating the process until the officer stopped moving. The reverberation from the strikes through Clifford's weapon lessened as he went from hitting bone to hitting something soft and wet. Car lights came at Clifford's back. He snapped his head to look over his shoulder. The patrol car and its flashing lights would block the person's view. Yet Clifford's rental car sat with its door open. Clifford stayed low and watched. The vehicle, some kind of small SUV, passed without slowing. He watched it grow smaller as it made its way up the street. He needed to move fast—every passing car would be another opportunity for someone to see that something was off. Clifford rose from the man's chest and went to the rental car's trunk. He pulled out his hatchet and went back to the cop.

CHAPTER 23

The repair of the truck had ended up taking only about twenty minutes, but after I got the Bronco back on the road, we had taken a half-hour drive and found us a little deserted road on the edge of the everglades. I took off the truck's top, and Amy laid the blanket over the backseat. We had our picnic under the stars and ended up spending a couple of hours talking with no phones, no television, and nothing to interrupt us. When we got home, Amy said something about it being one of our best dates. With my old Bronco not being the most reliable vehicle, I figured Amy and I could probably have similar dates in the future.

I was still thinking about our evening as I walked into my office the next morning and powered up my computer. The time was around seven thirty. My morning up to that point had been low-key. No one called waking me up with a homicide, no messages appeared on my phone about more murders overnight, and no one requested I get to a scene. I woke up without my alarm going off, had a few cups of coffee while I read the news reports on our investigation, said my goodbyes to Amy and Lucky, and went to work. Dave was on his phone when I walked past his office. I figured I'd check my email, let him finish up with his phone call, then pop over to see where he and his team had gotten with the case overnight. I powered up my computer and took a sip of my coffee that Amy sent me away with. Not ten seconds later, Dave burst into my office.

"He hit again," Dave said. "A patrol officer."

"What?" I snapped. "MDPD?"

Dave shook his head. "An officer from Miami Gardens PD named Pazanis. They obviously didn't know of the missing hand to make the connection and call us right away."

I set my coffee down and stood. "Give me the details."

"I guess it happened a couple hours ago. The last radio correspondence was that he was making a possible DUI stop. The plate he'd requested they run didn't match the vehicle. That was just before five this morning."

"What was the COD?" I asked.

"Blunt force trauma to the head, they figure. It was bad. There was also a couple of GSWs. And then there was the removal of the hand, so I guess it could have been a combination of things."

"Where was he shot?" I asked.

"Knee on the right leg, shin on the left."

"Where in Miami Gardens?" I asked.

"Over by the university off the Palmetto Expressway and Spartan Boulevard. Another patrol car went to where he last reported from when they couldn't get him on the radio. They found the officer's cruiser with the light bar, headlights, and spotlight on. The car was still running. The officer himself had been placed along the passenger side of the vehicle. Drag marks show how he'd been moved from the scene of whatever happened. There was blood evidence ahead of his cruiser by a car length or two."

"Whoever did it probably dragged him back to the patrol car so he wouldn't be as visible."

"I'd imagine something like that," Dave said.

"How did they know to call us?"

"Bert from the coroner's office."

The Bert that Dave referred to was Norberto Navarro, one of the county's night shift medical examiners.

Dave continued, "The officer had been deceased for a half hour or so by the time any paramedics were on scene. When the EMTs knew there was nothing they could do, they called the ME's office. Bert showed up to the scene and saw the missing hand. He told them that they needed to call us."

"What's going on at the scene? Do we know?" I asked.

"They still have a presence there," Dave said. "Their forensics team was looking over everything, but this may have to be a joint effort."

"Sure," I said. "One of their guys dead and our current investigation. Is the cap in yet?"

Dave shook his head. "I haven't seen him."

"Who were you talking to on the scene?"

"A Sergeant Houlihan," Dave said. "I told him that we'd have some people to the scene within the hour."

I got the time from my wrist. We were right in the gray area between the night shift ending and day shift starting.

"Are you sticking around?" I asked. "Or do you want to pass it off to us?"

"I want to go out to the scene, but I'll probably only be able to stay until we have a handle on it," he said. "Mary has her first job interview at ten. I have to make sure she's ready. Fatherly pre-interview pep talks and all."

"Sure," I said. "Where is she applying?"

"The grocery store down the street from our place. A couple of her friends work there. Seems like a decent after-school job."

"Cool," I said. "Whenever you need to go, say the word. I could probably call my guys in early if that's easier for you."

Dave waved away the offer. "I have an hour before my shift actually ends. That, and the scene is in the general direction of my house."

"Fair enough. Let me call Halloway and let him know what we have going on and make a quick call to Colt. Leave in five?"

"Works for me," Dave said. He started toward the bull pen to let his guys know they had a scene to be on. I dialed the captain then Colt. Halloway told me to call him with another update when we were on scene. Colt said he'd meet us on location as soon as he could.

I met up with Dave and his team, and in three unmarked cruisers, we left the station for Miami Gardens. Minus any traffic, the drive would have taken us about twenty minutes. At that time of the morning, though, even with the lights and sirens going, the traffic put our time closer to a half hour. Our three cars, nose to tail, exited off the Palmetto

Expressway and drove the half mile up to Spartan Boulevard. From the moment we exited, the university grounds sat behind a black metal fence on our right. Upon making our right turn, I spotted what looked like a roadblock and the lights of patrol cars roughly a quarter mile ahead. We'd found our scene. News vans, with masts in the air, lined the right shoulder of the road. Patrol cars were parked in front of the television crews. Blocking the street were a pair of marked Miami Gardens cruisers. Behind their cars were a couple of plastic barricades, and behind the barricades were more patrol cars. Dave led our group of cars and pulled to the left shoulder of the road. He parked on an angle with his front tires in the grass shoulder and his rear tires in the street. I pulled in beside him, and Malone and Burns pulled in beside me. We stepped from our cars and walked to the barricade blocking off the scene. A group of uniformed officers held the line.

"Miami Homicide," Dave said as we walked up.

"Cap," one of the officers called back over his shoulder.

A man in a suit talked with a couple of officers inside the barricade, looked toward us, and started our way.

"This is Captain Eland," the officer said. He turned toward the approaching captain. "Cap, these guys are Miami Homicide."

The captain waved us toward him, and we crossed the barricade.

We went through a round of introductions with Captain Eland. He said he'd just gotten on scene, and he spoke as he walked to the police cruiser that we were told had belonged to the deceased officer. A couple of guys in matching blue jackets, with big forensics patches across the back, rummaged around in the tree line beyond the patrol car. Standing on the far side of the car and watching the forensics guys work was a balding man wearing a Miami Gardens uniform. The guy looked somewhere in his later forties. His arms were crossed over his chest. The captain cleared his throat and pointed at the man in uniform. "This is Sergeant Houlihan," the captain said. "He should be able to answer everything you guys need."

The sergeant turned toward us. "Is one of you who I talked to?"

We again went through a quick round of introductions, with Dave saying that he was the one the sergeant had spoken to on the phone.

I stared at our scene—or what remained of it minus the officer's body. In front of the patrol car and marked with cones were a blood pool and drag marks that came toward us then disappeared from my view behind the front of the police cruiser. I took a few steps closer to the car and rounded the police cruiser's push bar on the front bumper. The drag marks stopped right along the passenger side of the car, where there was another pool of blood. I looked at the patrol car's windshield.

"Dash cam?" I asked.

"Our cars aren't equipped," Sergeant Houlihan said. He shook his head. "And I don't know how many times we'd requested budgeting for them."

"Was the car gone through?" I asked.

"Yeah. The computer is gone. And no, we don't have any way to track it. We'll have to have the crime lab go through it and see if they can find any evidence inside the cruiser. Speaking of which, what are we doing with the forensics side of this?"

"I have the lead of the Miami-Dade CSIS lab on his way," I said. "I'm guessing that the forensics guys on scene now can relay what they've found to him, and they can go from there."

"What can you tell us about the officer?" Dave asked.

"Tom Pazanis. Early forties. He was a transfer from Alabama. He'd only been with our department a couple months from what I heard. I saw him around the station during shift changes but didn't know too much of him. That bit I just gave you there was from our overnight patrol sergeant."

"He didn't normally share a car with anyone?" Dave asked.

Sergeant Houlihan shook his head. "We normally run one guy to a car. Another thing that frequently gets brought up during our budget meetings."

One of the forensics guys approached from the bushes beyond the grass shoulder of the road. He held a small black box on a cord in his hand. "We found his radio," the guy said.

"You said he called in the traffic stop?" Dave asked.

"Called in the plate to be run. The car being stopped was a late-model Chevy sedan, gold. The plate belonged to a different make and model vehicle. We ran the number and are in the process of contacting who it belongs to now," Houlihan said.

"I need that information," I said.

CHAPTER 24

Colt showed up around nine. I sent Dave and his guys off close to the same time. Colt had been talking with the forensics guys and was putting together the events of the attack. From the positioning of the blood, it seemed that the shooting happened between the vehicle that was pulled over and the nose of the patrol car. Meaning the suspect had already been out of the car. The blood then moved from the pavement into the grass, where it continued to the side of the patrol car. The scrappy grass and sand of the shoulder of the road was mostly red.

"Do you have the guys out knocking on doors?" Colt asked. He leaned against the tailgate of his truck, which he'd pulled through the police barricade closer to the scene. His pickup currently sat only ten feet or so away from the location of the vehicle that had been pulled over and left the scene. Colt stared at the camera he held. Its cord was wrapped around his neck.

"Yeah. None of these houses really have any kind of direct line of sight, though. Detective Ryan went north with one of the Miami Gardens patrol officers, Garcia went south with another officer. We know the vehicle was a gold-colored Chevy sedan. We're just trying to find someone who saw it pulled over last night."

"The plate didn't match up, though?" Colt asked.

I shook my head. "That's what I have Steve on. He's meeting up with Lieutenant Lopez and Detective Matan. They're making a house call on the address the plate comes back to. It's in Coral Gables. My guess would be they should be rolling up on that property shortly."

Colt stared at the screen on the back of the camera. He worked the buttons, probably going from one photo to the next.

"Scene photos?" I asked.

"Yeah. This is the Miami Gardens forensics guys' camera. The pics are from when they arrived at the scene." Colt waved me toward him and took the strap of the camera from around his neck. He passed me the camera and told me to use the left and right buttons on the sides of the screen to move from one photo to the next. "It's not pretty," Colt said. "They're bad."

I looped the camera strap around my neck and started going through the photos. The first was of blood on faded blacktop—two small pools then drag marks.

Colt looked over my shoulder at the photos.

"That's right in front of the cruiser. Where we figure he was shot in the legs."

I glanced at the blood on the ground just twenty feet from where I stood. The next couple of photos were of the drag marks themselves. Then came the photos of the body.

Colt was not exaggerating. They were bad. From the officer's neck up was nothing but red. His mouth hung open. Teeth were missing. His nose sat off to the side. The skin on his forehead was completely lacerated. The area of his forehead directly above his left eye was sunken in. The sand and grass beneath the officer's head was soaked in blood. I moved through the next few photos, which were close-ups of various facial wounds. An arm and wrist came into the camera's frame—no hand. Just as it was under the man's head, the ground was saturated in blood beneath the area where the hand had been removed. The ground had been disturbed beneath the wrist area from whatever chopped the hand off, like the scene with the prostitute, Kylie Bowe. After a few close-ups of the wrist area, the photos moved to the GSWs. The last few photos were of the inside of the patrol car, some spent shell casings on the ground, then the officer's service weapon and shoulder radio—they'd been found in the underbrush. I went through the photos a second time then passed the camera to Colt.

"Pretty savage attack," Colt said. He draped the camera strap over his head and let the camera hang from his neck.

"To say the least," I said. "Any clue on the murder weapon?"

"You mean what did that to his head and face?"

I nodded.

"I'd guess either the butt of the gun that shot him in the legs or the back end of the hatchet that took his hand."

"Does the area where the hand was removed from the wrist look the same as the other victims to you?" I asked.

"Looks damn near identical to the Kylie Bowe woman. And Town said that the wound on the guy from the shootout looked just like the wound from Bowe. We had a witness that said she saw the hand removal via hatchet, and I don't see any reason to not believe that was the same weapon used here."

I shook my head, deep in thought.

"What?" Colt asked.

"Nothing. Just no clue as to what in the hell we're dealing with here. I don't like it. We have reports of two different vehicles and a plate coming back to a third. We have a strangulation and beating on the prostitute, a straight-up gunfight on some street thugs and neighborhood residents while the guy is wearing armor, and now a shooting mixed with a beating on a cop. I don't see a connection or motive. The only connection at all, the only thing that comes close to tying one to the other, is the severed and missing hands."

"I know what you're saying. If the hands hadn't been removed, we wouldn't have a clue that we were dealing with the same person," Colt said. "But maybe the shooting of the officer here was done with one of the same weapons that was used during the shooting in Liberty City. The calibers match up. It's another connection if we can match the ballistics up, confirming the same weapon. Speaking of which, I sent the ballistics reports from the Liberty City scene over to Couch at the bureau. I haven't heard anything back yet."

"Okay," I said. "What do you have to do here?"

"I'm going to take my own photos of the car and the blood evidence on the ground. After that, a wrecker is going to come and grab the cruiser. Miami Gardens is going to take it back to their shop and relay whatever was found inside to me. Who knows, maybe we'll get lucky."

"All right. Let me call Steve and see what's shaking on this house call."

"Sure," Colt said. "Let me go find the owner of this camera and let him know that we need copies of every photo taken." Colt left the back of his truck in search of the Miami Gardens forensics team.

I pulled my phone from my pocket and dialed Steve. He answered on the second ring.

"Hey," Steve said.

"What did we come up with over there?" I asked.

"More questions," Steve said. "But maybe something we can run with."

"Let's hear it," I said.

"The owner of the car wasn't home at the registered address. A nineteen-year-old daughter was, though. She said her mother was at work and gave us the location, an office building just a couple miles away from the residence. So, we drive over to this office building, which is where we are now, and find the woman inside. We ask her about the plate, and of course, she doesn't have a clue. She walks us out to the parking structure and her car and shows it to us complete with a plate on the back. Except the plate isn't one she recognizes. We run that tag to find out it comes back to a 2012 Ford and the plate was reported stolen yesterday."

"Stolen from where?" I asked.

"The owner figures the Mall of Americas by Fountainebleau."

"Did you ask the woman if she was there since yesterday?"

"We did, and she was there yesterday. That's what we're working with her on now. We're trying to get a satellite map of the mall up on one of the computers at her work so she can show us where she was parked. Maybe we can catch the plate swapping on some security footage."

"It's something," I said. "Good work."

"We'll see what pans out. What's going on there?"

"Not much left to the scene to look at. Some blood evidence and a couple shell casings. I looked at some photos of the scene with the officer still present. Pretty rough sight. You said Mall of Americas?"

"Yeah."

"Let me see what if anything Garcia or Ryan got. If we're a bust out here, I may just gather up the troops and come and meet you over at the mall. I assume that's going to be your next stop."

"It is. I would think that we'll probably be in that area within a half hour or so."

"All right. I'll call you back when we head out."

"Sounds good," Steve said.

CHAPTER 25

Doing his damnedest to wipe his prints from anything he touched, Clifford ransacked the cop's car before he left the scene. He was looking for any kind of dash cam or recording device inside the car. He found nothing. The only thing of interest was what the cop had plugged into his computer—the stolen tag number and the make, model, and color of Clifford's rental car.

Clifford wasn't going to take any chances that the cop had entered more information than what now appeared on the screen—or that there was a camera somewhere and the computer had been recording footage. Clifford yanked the computer from the car and tossed it into the first water he found upon leaving the traffic stop. In case the computer could be tracked, he wanted it out of his possession immediately. Tossing it in a pond, he thought, was a hell of a lot better idea than smashing it. A smashed computer still gave the county's tech team a crack at getting whatever the computer had. But when it was sunk thirty feet down in a neighborhood pond, Clifford wished them luck with their retrieval.

Clifford shook his head. Again, he leaned back in his recliner. The news played as it had the prior morning. The wound on his arm seeped a bit of blood, his body ached from the bullets he'd taken through his body armor, and a smell of something cooking wafted from the kitchen. He felt as if he was in a loop, no further ahead than he was the day before.

Beside him on the table were a bunch of bones from the hand of one of the men he'd shot in the street. Clifford was in no rush to get them assembled and displayed. He was awash in disappointment. The cop, the man he'd just beaten to death with the butt of his pistol, was supposed to have been the pinnacle of his achievement, his most capable prey. The guy didn't even fight back. He didn't get a shot off. He didn't hit Clifford with a Taser, and there was no heated hand-to-hand fight. Nothing. Nothing that Clifford had imagined had happened. The guy just died. The hooker had put up more resistance. The cop simply wasn't prepared to deal with him.

He put his fingers into the hair that remained on the back of his head, scratched a bit, then brought his hand over his head's bald top. Out of nowhere, he wondered why he hung on to the little hair that remained on the sides and back. The last time he went to get a trim, the woman asked him if he wanted to throw in the towel and she'd give him a nice lather, hot towel, and shave. Clifford remembered feeling insulted at the time, but the truth was he'd completely balded on the top, just like his father before him. The timer in the kitchen sounded, breaking him from his daydreaming about his hair. Clifford rose from his chair, walked to the pot on the stove, and clicked the burner off. He took a quick look into the pot and gave it a stir with a wooden spoon.

He snatched a bowl from the kitchen cupboard and a big spoon from the drawer next to the refrigerator. Clifford filled his bowl from the pot and grabbed a sleeve of crackers that he had set out. He took everything to his kitchen table, sat, and plunged the spoon into the bowl of chicken noodle soup. Clifford filled the spoon with some of the broth and brought it to his lips. He blew and sipped the soup.

CHAPTER 26

"We found one person who heard the shots," Garcia said. "They live in a house on the next block north and a couple houses in from the road the shooting took place on. They saw nothing. Just claimed they heard a pair of shots."

"So, we've got squat aside from another dead body?" Steve asked. "A dead body that's a cop," he added.

"Did we ever get word back if the FBI had anything matching up with the ballistics on this?" Ryan asked.

"Colt said he hadn't heard anything back yet," I said. I leaned against the back of my unmarked patrol car in the mall parking lot. Garcia and Ryan's cruiser was parked directly next to mine. Steve's car was straight across the aisle. We'd all arrived at the mall a few minutes prior. Colt had remained at the scene by the university, waiting on the tow truck that would take the police cruiser. The Miami Gardens PD was going to keep door knocking throughout the day and relay anything of substance to us.

"We're just waiting on Wade?" I asked.

"I called and asked him to meet us over here," Steve said. "When I called the office here at the mall, they agreed to let us have a look at the security feeds, no paperwork required. I figured getting Tech out here right away with something to make us a copy of the footage would help in the interest of saving time. Then we wouldn't have to wait for Tech to coordinate on coming here to make copies."

"Sure," I said. "So, he was on his way?"

"That's what he said, yeah," Steve said.

"Okay. I need to make a quick phone call. Why don't you guys head in and contact whoever you have to. Get the ball rolling. Wade can meet everyone inside when he gets here."

"I suppose. Find the office, find who we need to talk to. Are you calling Halloway?" Steve asked.

"Yeah," I said.

Steve gave me a nod, and he, Ryan, and Garcia walked to the mall's entrance. I took a seat in my car and dialed the captain.

"Halloway," he answered.

"Hey, Cap," I said. "It's Harrington."

"What's going on out there?" he asked.

I gave him a rundown of what we had on scene.

"And you never found anything to connect the guys from Liberty City to the prostitute?"

"The only connection was they were both breaking the law. The guys pushing drugs and the girl soliciting. Yet the neighborhood residents weren't breaking the law, and they took fire. We have one complete innocent bystander that died, so I don't know if committing a crime is any kind of connection. When you factor in the latest victim, a police officer, that possible connection becomes even weaker."

"How was the scene?" Halloway asked.

"The officer's body had been removed by the time I got there, but I saw the photos of the scene, and the blood evidence remained. Looks like he was shot in the legs, dragged behind his car, and bludgeoned to death."

"Good God," Halloway said. "I don't suppose we found a murder weapon?"

"Nothing on location," I said.

The captain let out a long breath. "And now you guys are at the mall, trying to hunt down video?"

"Yeah. Hopefully we can see the plates getting swapped from one car to the other. We have a general area where the woman said she'd parked."

"Okay. When you guys are done there, call me. I want to get everyone in the conference room and put everything we have up on the boards so we can look at it."

"All right," I said. "I'll let you know when we're headed back."

"Sounds good," Halloway said. He clicked off.

I stepped from the car and dialed Steve. He picked up after a couple of rings and guided me to the mall's security office, where he and the guys were. I walked down the hallway toward the restrooms by the food court and pushed open the door at the back of the hallway. After I passed through, the door clanked shut at my back. Another hallway stretched ahead of me. The walls and floor were white and stark. A few doors down, one of the doors to my right was open. My guys were inside. Garcia and Ryan stood with a man in a security guard's uniform.

I'd found the security office. The room was fifteen by fifteen feet and had no windows—just computer monitors. A U-shaped desk spanned the left, back, and right walls. Above the wraparound desk, each wall of the room had two sixty-some-inch monitors bolted to it. Each monitor showed what looked like ten or more security feeds from various parts of the mall. I could see people walking about inside and cars moving in and out of parking spots outside. Below each monitor was a computer workstation holding two additional monitors and a big clunky looking keyboard with a joystick. There was a total of six stations. Steve sat next to another man dressed in a guard's uniform at the station farthest right and closest to the door.

I gave the sill of the door a knock.

Steve looked over his shoulder and waved me toward him. "We're just getting everything pulled up now."

I walked over and stood next to Detective Ryan.

"Everything will come up on this monitor here," the seated security guard said. He pointed at the big monitor bolted to the wall above his workstation. "I just need a time and location."

Steve had a piece of paper in front of him. It looked like a printed photo of an aerial view of the mall. "This is where she said she parked," Steve said. He showed the security officer on the map. "Yesterday. The woman said she was at the mall from around six until seven thirty."

"All right. Give me just a second," the security officer said. He looked at the map then started punching away at his computer. "It looks like lot camera forty-two probably catches that area there. What vehicle are we looking for?"

"A black 2012 Ford Taurus or a bright red 2015 Honda Fit," Steve said.

"Keep your eyes open for a gold-colored Chevy as well," I said.

"Well, let's see what we got." The guard punched away at his computer then pointed up. "This is six o'clock yesterday," he said.

I looked over the footage of the parking lot displayed on the screen. Lines of cars ran up the left and right side of the monitor. The quality was okay at best. The vehicles could be segmented as light, dark, car, or truck, though I couldn't say that I saw anything that would qualify as bright red.

"Is this as good as the quality gets?" Ryan asked.

"This is what we have to work with," the security guard said.

I watched as a car came into view at the bottom of the monitor. The car was moving toward the back of the parking lot, away from the camera. We had as good a view of the license plate as we were going to get, and I couldn't make out a single letter or number. I shook my head but said nothing. Even if we caught anything on camera, the quality wasn't good enough for us to do anything with it.

"Hopefully Wade can do something to clean this footage up," Steve said.

Steve had voiced exactly what I and probably the rest of the guys were thinking.

"Here's a red car. Looks like a little hatchback," Ryan said. "Could be our Honda."

"Looks like it, yeah," I said. The car made a Y-turn and backed into a parking spot. A moment later, we saw a woman emerge from where the car was parked and walk toward the camera. "Is that the woman you went and talked to?" I asked.

"Looks like it's probably her, from what I can tell. The build is the same. Hair looks about the same. Again, from what I can tell from this," Steve said.

The woman walked out of the camera's frame.

"Do we have her contact information?" I asked.

"I have it, yeah," Steve said.

"Give her a call and see if she backed in," I said. "Seems an odd thing to do at a mall. Or at least enough out of the ordinary that she may remember."

"Sure. Let me try her." Steve rose from his chair and left the security office while he made the call.

I looked over the rest of the vehicles parked near the red hatchback. A couple were darker and could have possibly been our Ford. I glanced at the time on the security footage—a few minutes before seven. We continued to watch the footage. A few people had come into the camera's frame, got in their vehicles, and left. A few more came.

Steve walked back into the office. He was tucking his cell phone into the inner chest pocket of his suit jacket. "She says she always backs in at malls. Something about a car backing into her while she was backing out years ago."

"Okay, it's pretty safe to assume that was her, then."

Steve nodded.

We went back to watching the cars pull in and out. At

ten after seven, we saw what might have been our Chevy come slowly into the top of the security camera's frame. The vehicle seemed to be moving slower than the other cars that had been coming and going, almost as if they were looking for something. The Chevy made a Y-turn, as the Honda did, and backed in a few spots away from it. We waited for someone to emerge and walk toward the mall entrance. Minutes passed, and no one did. At seven eighteen, the car pulled out from the parking spot and left in the direction it came. We had a clear look at the back of the car, yet we weren't going to be able to make out any kind of plate.

"Looks like a light-colored Malibu," Garcia said. "Silver or gold. That's got to be our car, and our guy."

"Call Wade," I said to Steve. "Get an ETA."

Steve made the call.

"Is there any other camera that would catch this area here?" I asked. "Maybe the camera that catches the next row of cars over?"

"Let me pull up forty-one and see what we get," the security officer said. He clicked away at his computer for a moment and brought up another camera feed. The right-hand side would be where whatever was going down would have taken place.

"This is the exact same time?" I asked.

He confirmed.

We sat and watched the footage but never spotted anyone doing anything. The Honda was nowhere in frame, and a full-size van was doing its best to block the view of where we figured the Chevy had parked.

"Can we go back to the other footage and maybe try to follow that Chevy in and out of the lot?" Garcia asked. "See where it comes from and which direction it leaves?"

The security guard shook his head. "In real time we can pan out and move the cameras. On the recorded footage, what you see is what we have."

CHAPTER 27

We left the mall around noon. Wade made a copy of the footage that the camera picked up and said he would try a few things to clean it up. I wasn't sure how much it would even matter. We had a vehicle that pulled in and pulled out. Using what was reported by the officer who was killed, combined with what we saw on the footage, we had the vehicle as a 2016 or 2017 Chevy Malibu, color gold. We never saw a plate on the vehicle while it pulled in, and the only thing cleaning up the footage was going to do was confirm that the car left with the plate from the Honda. There was no camera view of our suspect. When I got back to the station, I had a voicemail waiting in my office. Couch had left a message that they'd gone through the ballistics reports and come up blank after running the images of the bullet striations through their system. He said if we needed the bureau to look into anything else, to feel free to call.

I gave Halloway's office door a knock and walked in. He sat at his desk, staring at his computer.

"How did we do at the mall?" he asked. The captain didn't take his eyes from his computer screen. He pointed at the guest chair across from him.

"Wade is trying to do some magic with the footage, but I don't think we're going to get much from it either way," I said. I walked to his desk and pulled out a seat. "We never get a view of the car pulling in to try to get a plate from it, and we never see the driver out of the car."

"Late model Chevy?" Halloway asked. He still didn't look at me. Whatever was on his computer had most of his attention.

"Sixteen or seventeen Malibu. Gold," I said. "Not really sure if that's something that we can put out a BOLO for. My guess is that there are quite a few in the area."

"Don't care. We're going to do it, anyway." Halloway leaned forward and grabbed the top edge of his computer monitor. He spun it so I could see the screen. I caught only the headline of the article, but it was all that I needed. The article was on the website for one of the main daily Miami papers. The headline read: *Murder and Dismemberment in Liberty City*. The first line of the article said something about a person witnessing the killer using a hatchet to take a hand from a victim.

I cracked my neck from one side to the other. "It looks like the woman from the shooting in Liberty City started flapping her gums to the press," I said. "How long has that article been out?"

"About a half hour," Halloway said. "I got a call from the brass upstairs. Apparently, the station has started getting calls from news outlets looking for us to comment on the article. Which means that comment or not, they'll run with this as a story by this evening. Needless to say, we need to get something together and get ahead of it. The press will dig deeper into that removal of the hand. They'll find out this wasn't the only instance."

"All right," I said.

"Is everyone here? Can we round everyone up?"

"Yeah. Let me grab the guys from the bull pen and make a call downstairs to Wade and Colt."

"I'll call Mark," the captain said. "Conference room in ten minutes."

I left Halloway's office, rounded everyone up, and made my phone calls. We assembled in the big conference room in our department. Steve sat across from Garcia and Ryan at the conference table. Colt sat on the file cabinet near the coffee station. He pushed his glasses up the bridge of his nose and stared down at a piece of paper that he held. I filled a cup of coffee and had a seat at Steve's side. Mark Swanson, the station's PR guy, sat on the far end of the table, away from everyone else. He wore a suit with a white dress shirt and patterned red tie. His dark hair was parted on the side. I always thought he looked more like a salesman than a public relations exec. I guessed there wasn't much difference. His job was to sell the public on what we were giving them. Wade was the last person that we were waiting on. He walked in with a folder tucked under his arm and had a seat next to Detective Ryan.

"We're all here?" Halloway asked.

I figured the question was rhetorical since we were.

Halloway stood in front of the big whiteboard farthest

left in the room. He looked from one person to the other while he tapped the end of a dry erase marker against his palm. Steve and I turned in our chairs and faced him. The captain had previously mentioned something about his wife putting him on a diet, and as I looked at him, his success was beginning to show. His normally round cheeks were not quite as round, and he seemed to have more room than usual in the waist of his suit jacket. Halloway popped the top off the marker with his teeth. "Let's jump right in," he said. The captain wrote the word "victims" on the top of the board.

"Kylie Bowe," I said. "Prostitute. Body found a few blocks from Seventy-Ninth and Biscayne."

The captain wrote the information down. The marker he used squeaked on the whiteboard as he moved from one letter to the next.

"Five at Liberty City," Steve said. "Three drug dealers. One armed resident. One innocent bystander."

Halloway wrote that down. "Names?"

Steve rattled them all off.

"And which one had the hand removed?" the captain asked.

"LaShawn Robinson," I said.

The captain made a check mark next to the name. "The officer's name?" he asked. Halloway held the marker to the board while he waited.

"Thomas Pazanis," I said. "Miami Gardens PD."

Halloway jotted the name at the bottom of the list. "And we have absolutely nothing to connect these people? Have we looked into everything?"

"Not that we know of," I said. "I kind of touched on it with you before. There's just nothing."

"I want someone on it either way," Halloway said. "I don't want to find out that there is a connection after the fact. We need to dig as deep as we can."

"I'll see what I can find," Garcia said. "I'll run the names of each vic past any friends or family of the other vics that we can get ahold of. I'll cross-reference whatever I can find of past addresses, employers, schools, etcetera."

The captain moved to the next whiteboard. "What do we know about our suspect?" he asked.

"Average height, average weight," I said.

"Body armor," Steve said. "Top to bottom. Wearing a mask. Reports that he took gunfire to the face, so ballistic in nature if the witnesses' accounts are to be believed."

"Okay," Halloway said. "Where can you buy a ballistic mask?"

"Probably a bunch of places online," I said.

"If he took a shot to the face and walked it off, it has to be some real armor," Ryan said. "Not some airsoft garbage. The real ballistic face masks aren't that common. I bet there's only a handful of places that sell them and probably few that are actually ordered."

"Let me check it out," Steve said. "I'll see what I can find as far as sales outlets and make some phone calls."

"Look locally too," I said.

"Sure," Steve said.

"Vehicles?" the captain asked.

"Driving either a big SUV or a gold Chevy Malibu," Ryan said.

"Land Rover Defender from what the woman pointed out," I said. "We put a BOLO out on it last night. Though that's just going by a witness account. You know how people can be with vehicles. We can spend a month searching for this Land Rover and then find out it was a Jeep."

"Is there a way we can search the DMV records to see if we have both of those vehicles registered to one party?" Ryan asked.

"The truck, if it was in fact what the woman pointed out, would probably be rare enough in itself," I said. "Yet you can't search the DMV database by vehicle."

"I can't believe that in this day and age, there's still not a way to do that," Wade said. "I could probably make two phone calls and find someone who could write a program in ten minutes that could do it. Yet we'd need access to the DMV database, which we won't get."

"Let's not worry about what we can't do," Halloway said. "You said the truck is rare?"

"Very," I said.

"Then the owner is probably an enthusiast. Check the forums, search online. Find someone in the area who owns one."

"I got it," Ryan said. "What exactly is it?"

"Either a ninety-three Land Rover Defender 110 or some kind of gray market one of a different year. That is the model, though. Witnesses say it had a roof rack. Big tires."

"Gray market?" Ryan asked.

"The specific truck the witness ID'd was only for sale here in the US one year," I said. "That was 1993. If it's any other year, it's over twenty-five years old and had to have been imported."

"And dark in color from what we know?" Ryan asked.

"That's what we got, yeah," I said.

"Okay. I'll search around online and see if I can find a community of local owners."

"Perfect," Halloway said. "And we think this guy is injured, correct?"

"We had blood on the scene in Liberty City," Colt said. "Whatever the injury was, obviously he was still capable of taking out a police officer."

"Okay. So injured, but not something that is life threatening." Halloway wrote "minor injury" on the board. "Anything else on our guy?"

No one responded.

"Okay," Halloway said. He moved to the top of the next whiteboard. "Irons in the fire. Aside from checking into the truck and the ballistic mask, what do we have that we're working on?"

"The guy hasn't really given us much in the way of evidence left behind," Colt said. "All the spent shell casings have been fingerprint free. I'm still waiting on a cast to be made from the wrists of the victims where the hands had been severed. Maybe I'll get with Skip and try to arrange something for me to pop over there and get it done. We have a witness that says a hatchet was used, but I'd like proof of that either way. Let's see. What else." Colt stared down at the paper that he held. "The blood for a DNA match still has to be processed," he said. "That's going to be a bit of a wait to get results if he is in the system somewhere. Once complete, it will give us a profile to reference. We also have the bullet ballistics that we still need to check. See if one of the same weapons from Liberty City was used on the slain officer."

"What about the officer's car?" I asked.

"I haven't heard anything from Miami Gardens on it yet," Colt said. "I can call them."

"All right," Halloway said. "Wade, what can we do with that video we just picked up? Anything?"

I looked over at Wade. He seemed unsure.

"What we got from the mall really isn't going to do much for us, unfortunately," Wade said. "But I was thinking. That's a super high traffic area with businesses galore. We have a time that this guy was in that area, so maybe I can try to touch base with other businesses and see if we picked his car up somewhere else."

"Okay. Do that and see what you get," Halloway said.

"Guys," Mark said. He lifted his hand to get our attention. He tapped the tip of his pen on the paper that was before him on the conference table. "What are we planning on saying, if anything, about the severed hand or hands?"

"Lay it all out for them. Tell the press we have three victims. But stay away from the word *trophies*," Halloway said. "Or mementos, or keepsakes, or anything that sounds like that. Let's just confirm that, yes, hands were severed in three instances, but we don't know why and we're currently working on finding out. Maybe throw something in there about not speculating on a reason. If we give the trophies thing life, this whole thing is going to spiral into a big nightmare in the press."

"That might be something that's out of our control," Mark said. "I don't know how the hell I'm going to spin random people being murdered and hands being chopped off and taken. I'm not sure I can turn that into anything other than what it is."

"Try," Halloway said.

CHAPTER 28

The straight razor being dragged over his scalp sounded like sandpaper in his head. With each swipe, Clifford could feel his skin pulling and sliding along his skull. The woman shaving him wiped the shaving cream from the razor on a towel and went back for another swipe. Clifford was reclined in the barber's chair. He stared at the television. A replay of the footage from Liberty City was airing on the news. Clifford had seen it a few times already. The part was coming up where the reporter questioned the broad-chested suit-wearing cop with the brown buzz cut. Clifford closed his eyes and sank into thought to the sounds of hair being scraped from his scalp.

His disappointment from killing the cop hadn't subsided. It was like kicking a puppy. Clifford had had a mental image of how the altercation was going to go down. He'd imagined going blow for blow, or shot for shot, with the cop. He figured there would be a physical battle. Ingrained in his head was the vision of himself narrowly escaping but victorious. He'd be beaten and bloodied—injured, even—but would have proven his mettle and have his proof of conquest with the cop's hand as a trophy. Clifford shook his head.

"Sir," the woman said.

Clifford opened his eyes.

She chuckled and held the razor so he could see it. "Remember that bit I told you about telling me if you had to sneeze or cough or get an itch or move?"

"What?" he asked.

"You kind of shook your head. I think I nicked you a bit."

"Oh, sorry," he said. "I was thinking about something."

"You don't have to apologize to me. I just don't want you to jump in your chair and your ear land on the floor."

"I'll hold still," he said.

"All right. I'm almost done. A couple more passes. Let me get this, though."

Clifford saw her grab the corner of her towel and dab at something on the side of his head—blood, he figured. He again heard the razor scraping across his scalp on the back of it.

"Have you seen this on the news?" she asked. "The guy killing people."

"Yeah," Clifford said.

"Now they're saying that he's cutting off the hands of the people he kills and keeping them. What a psycho," she said. "Who the hell would do that?"

"If you're a hunter and you kill a giant buck, you get it mounted, right? The same goes if you're a fisherman and catch the fish of a lifetime. People fill their homes and cottages and lodges and cabins with the stuff. I imagine this is no different."

"Except whoever the hell this is happens to be murdering people and cutting off their hands as opposed to catching a big fish and having it mounted," the man in the neighboring chair said. The woman spritzing the man's hair with water and using a scissors to trim it seemed to agree, voicing a long *mmm-hmm*.

"Touché," Clifford said.

"I hope they catch the guy," the hairdresser shaving Clifford's head said. Earlier, she'd said that her name was Tiffany. "Catch him, lock him up, throw away the key."

"It doesn't sound like they have much," the man sitting next to Clifford said. "Which means they probably ain't going to find the guy unless he wants to be found."

"What do you mean wants to be found?" Tiffany asked.

"Some of these psychos, that's what they're after. They want the cops to chase them. They want the fame and recognition. Probably losers in real life and this is the only way they can be someone of importance."

The guy continued talking, but Clifford had tuned him out. Yet part of what the guy said continued to reverberate through his head. It was the "they want the cops to chase them" part. Clifford thought about the cop he killed, the men he shot in Liberty City, the prostitute. All the victims shared one thing—they were unprepared for his attack. They weren't ready. He was the hunter and they were the prey. Clifford thought of the people he'd killed and who the biggest adversary had been—it took him only a second. The homeowner who came at him with the shotgun had been the only real threat. And that homeowner was a threat only because he knew what the situation was and had made a conscious decision to act. He saw what was going on, armed himself, and came outside with the goal of putting Clifford down.

Clifford pursed his lips in thought. Maybe presenting an officer with someone to chase would provide a better adversary when the pair came face to face. His eyes went back to the television screen. The big-chested cop in a suit was asking for the public's help. An idea began to form in Clifford's freshly shaved head.

Tiffany, the hairdresser, planted a mirror in front of Clifford's face. "What do you think?" she asked.

Clifford glanced at his reflection yet was too deep in thought to care very much about his newfound baldness. He glanced at the cop on the television. Beneath the man's image, it said *Liberty City* and *Sergeant Walsh, Miami Homicide Bureau* on a banner across the bottom of the screen. "It's perfect," Clifford said.

CHAPTER 29

After the press conference, I touched base with everyone. Ryan had found a pair of truck forums that had local members and sent a couple of emails to the forum moderators—he was waiting to hear something. Garcia still searched for a single connection between the vics. Steve was looking into the mask and apparently had found a number of sales outlets that he'd left messages for. Wade couldn't do anything with the mall footage we had but planned to go out in the field in search of more video the next morning. Colt was waiting on the bullets from the slain officer to arrive from our county medical examiner's office. I filled Dave in on our day and headed home a little after six.

The only peep I heard from my phone the entire night was a text from Colt saying that they didn't find any prints in the officer's cruiser that didn't belong to Pazanis. They did say that the car could have been wiped down.

I welcomed a night where I wasn't working five hours past the end of my shift or wakened to go back in three hours before my shift started, but it also meant that nothing was breaking on the investigation. I got my fill of binge watching

TV and listening to Amy talk about her coworkers. I was in bed by midnight. I'd called Dave when I woke up to see if we had any updates. He said that there hadn't been anything new to report. He had Burns and Malone weeding through the calls that had come in on the tip line that we'd set up, but nothing seemed too promising.

I walked into our department a few minutes after eight o'clock, having just come from the lunchroom. I'd gotten to the office about a half hour earlier. Steve must have shown up while I was making short work of a blueberry Danish down the hall. He sat at his desk, and I headed over.

"Morning," I said.

"What's up? What happened overnight?" Steve asked.

"Not much, thankfully, or unfortunately, depending on your take on things. Thankfully no new murders, unfortunately no new leads to chase down."

"Nothing came into the phone lines?"

"I guess Malone and Burns were manning them overnight. Nothing of substance to report."

"Damn. Well, we'll see. Our press conference played on the morning news, so hopefully we keep getting calls the more they show it."

I nodded, took a sip of my coffee, and sat down in one of Steve's guest chairs. "Anything new on the mask?"

He shook his head. "There are more places than I thought that sell them. On top of that, you have the used market as well. Seems that there are a couple of places that manufacture them, but then, like anything, they ship to distributors and from there to the sales outlets. Thinking about it now, I've actually seen these things at gun shows and shit as well."

"So, a bust?"

"I'm still waiting on some callbacks. I found a couple local places that sell them, or at least have sold them in the past. We'll see what shakes out there. I did learn a bit more about them, though."

"What's that?" I asked.

"That I doubt our guy took a straight shot to the head if he was wearing one. And if he did, he's probably not doing so well. From what I hear, it's more of a save-your-life kind of thing, but you're still headed to the hospital with broken bones in your face."

"Glancing shot, maybe."

"Maybe," Steve said. "Probably still shows the signs of it, though."

I nodded. Our description went from average size and weight guy of unknown age and race to the same with possible facial injuries. I guessed it was something.

"What's up with you? Anything new?" Steve asked.

I didn't have anything new on the case to kick around with him, yet there was something that had been on my mind. It had started the prior night and continued that morning. Getting his take on it might help clear things up. "Not on the case, but I have something that I want to run by you."

"Shoot," Steve said.

"Remember a couple months ago when Amy was having Sasha ask you to ask me about marriage?" I asked.

"Yeah," he said. "Why?"

"Has she said anything else to Sasha about the topic lately?"

"Don't know. Not that I heard. Why?" he asked. "Are you going to ask her now? Wondering if she's still interested?"

I waved away his question. "Okay. All I needed to know."

"Nah. Not that easy. Spill it. What's with the question?" Steve asked.

"Just a weird talk that we were having last night, and I'm not sure if she was trying to drop hints or what the hell was up with it."

"What was the talk?" Steve asked.

"Well, we were binge watching some television show. About the third episode in, she pauses the TV to fill me in on the goings-on of one of the managers that works for her. She says she approved a couple weeks of vacation for the woman so she could have a destination wedding. Somewhere in the Caribbean or something. Then off on a boat to another tropical island for a week's worth of staying in some cabin thing on the ocean for the honeymoon. She just kept going on about it. She was asking if I thought that was a cool idea. Asking how I felt about that as opposed to a traditional wedding. Things like that."

"Have you ever met this employee of hers?"

"Never," I said. "I've never even heard her name mentioned before. I think she said it was Bridget."

"You mean her name was Bullshit," Steve said.

He might have been right.

"What else did she say about the employee?" Steve asked.

I furrowed my brow. "Amy said that the guy this manager was marrying had popped the question on their two-year anniversary. Which I thought an odd detail."

Steve laughed. "I got five that says the woman doesn't exist."

As much as I didn't want to think that my girlfriend was stringing together some fiction in an attempt to subliminally message me, I wasn't going to take the bet. I stuck my palm in my eye.

"You should probably just ask her," Steve said. "Just throw in the towel, give up, and submit."

"Well, when you put it like that…"

"Hey!" I heard. I glanced past Steve to see the captain leaning out of his office door. Steve turned in his chair to look over his shoulder. The captain's face and body language didn't look as if he was too pleased with something. He waved us over. "Both of you," he said and disappeared back into his office.

"That didn't look good," Steve said. He stood from his chair.

"Nah, it didn't," I said. I stood, scooped up my coffee from the corner of Steve's desk, and followed him across the bull pen and into the captain's office.

"Sit," Halloway said. His computer monitor was turned sideways on his desk. He seemed to have a video paused on the screen.

"What's going on?" I asked.

"I just got three phone calls in a row asking me for a comment on this."

Halloway clicked his computer mouse and leaned back in his chair.

VESTIGE

It appeared as if the video was embedded in an email. The footage panned across what looked like some kind of rock fireplace mantel. The mantel held a few glass boxes. Inside the boxes were the skeletal remains of human hands on red velvet pillows.

"What the hell is this?" I asked.

Halloway held up his hand for me to hold my question.

"I'm a hunter," a man's voice on the video said. "An apex predator. The top of the food chain. The tip of the pyramid. I have yet to find a creature on this earth to best me, be it man or beast. My home is filled with the mounts of my conquests. Beasts from every continent. From the frozen tundra to the desert sands. Yet these are my most prized possessions." The camera panned over the skeletal hands again. "A small reminder of my superiority over another of God's most deadly creatures—man. There is room on my mantel. Sergeant Walsh from the Miami Police, I have a display case with your name on it. I'm coming for you. Be ready."

The video ended.

Steve said nothing.

"Call Sasha," I said. "Tell her not to go home."

"What?" Steve asked.

"Sasha, make sure she doesn't go home," I said. "Send her to my house. Amy is there. Where is she now? At work?"

"Yeah," Steve said. He snapped out of his daze. "Let me call her." Steve stood from the captain's desk while he held his phone to his ear.

"Where the hell did this video come from?" I asked.

Halloway let out a big puff of air. "Originally, I don't know.

This was emailed over to me from a reporter at the *Daily Gazette*. The guy was looking for a comment. While I was talking to him and he was emailing this, I got calls from channels six and ten. It looks like everyone got copies of this."

"The video was sent to the papers and television?" I asked.

"Yeah," Halloway said.

Steve took his seat again. "She doesn't answer," he said. "She never does at work, though. Let me send her a text." He tapped away with his thumbs on his phone's screen.

"Any clue why your name is on this video, Walsh?" Halloway asked.

Steve shrugged. "No," he said. He looked confused. He shook his head. "What the hell would this nut want with me?"

"Good question," the captain said. "You can't think of anyone over the years that you've dealt with that you can attribute this kind of shit to?"

"No," Steve said. "Not even close."

"Well, he's got eyes on you for one reason or another," I said. "I don't imagine that he just picked your name out of a hat."

"You think it was from the reporter interviewing me on the scene?" Steve asked.

"Maybe," I said. "Who was in front of the cameras? Just you and Chestnut?"

"I think, yeah," Steve said. "I answered a couple questions that a reporter was firing off at me. How the hell does that make me a target of this guy?"

"You're getting a babysitter," Halloway said. "A couple of them. And don't give me any shit about it."

Steve didn't respond.

"Let's get Wade on the line. See what the hell he can do about finding where that video originally came from," I said.

"Good idea," Halloway said. "Call him." He scooped up his phone. My guess was that he was calling someone over in Patrol about getting some shadows for Steve.

Steve simply sat in the captain's desk chair. I could see the concern on his face as he tried to figure out what exactly was making him a target of this guy.

I dialed Wade down in Tech. Hopefully he could get us some answers on the footage.

CHAPTER 30

Within the hour, the footage began to play on every channel—even the ones that had told Mark from our PR department that they wouldn't replay it. There was nothing that we could do to stop it from spreading like a virus through the press. Steve's name was scrolling across the bottom of every local news broadcast.

We'd watched the footage numerous times. The station's phones were ringing nonstop from people looking to get a response out of him and our department. Steve appeared more annoyed than anything. Yet I knew deep down that he was well aware how credible the threat was. We knew the guy was capable of murder. We knew he was well armed and had no qualms about taking an officer's life. The fact that this guy had made a target of Steve didn't sit right with me. Our suspect was taking his act to a new level that we weren't prepared for.

"I've got nothing," Garcia said. He walked into my office with a stack of papers in his hand.

I sat at my desk with Steve across from me. Steve held the phone to his ear, having just gotten Sasha on the line.

I waved Garcia in.

"I can't find any connection between these victims. Completely random from what I can tell," Garcia said. "I spent three hours last night on the phones and another one now with the people I didn't make contact with or needed to try back. If these vics were connected in any way, I'd be floored."

"Okay," I said. I pointed at his papers. "What's this?"

"The vics and sheets for everyone that I've contacted. Friends and family," Garcia said.

I took the papers from him and set them on my desk. "Do you know if Ryan was getting anywhere on those forums?" I asked.

"Someone got back to him. I guess they put him on a local social media group for owners. He said he was trying to hunt down the guy who runs that group."

"Good," I said.

"What do you want me on now?"

"Go check in with Wade. See what he's getting from the video."

"You got it," Garcia said. He turned and left my office.

Steve clicked off from his call a moment later. "She's at your house," Steve said. "Scared. The news reports have her all spun up."

I nodded, not having much of a response for him.

"Thanks for putting us up," Steve said. "We could have probably gone out to her parents', but honestly, that would have sucked."

I smiled "No problem. You guys are always welcome with

Amy and me. Are you going to have to run to your house after work?"

"Yeah. I'll pack up a bag for Sasha and me then head over to your house. Cap said he was going to send a car with me to go out there."

"I'll just go with you," I said. "No point in pulling someone else off patrol when you and I are going to end up at the same place, anyway."

"That's fine. So, what's our next move?" Steve asked.

"Hopefully finding something on that video to go on," I said. "Wade said he was going to try to find out who got it first at each news outlet. If we can find out where the video file was originally sent from, we'll be in business," I said.

"If," Steve said.

"Well, it's something." My desk phone rang. I reached out and scooped it up. "Harrington," I answered.

"Hey, it's Colt. We've got a match here on the bullets. Skip got me everything I needed right when I got in. Confirmed that it's one of the same weapons from Liberty City that was used to shoot the officer at Miami Gardens."

"Okay," I said. It was something that we'd already been pretty much set on, but it was confirmation of the fact nonetheless. "What have you got to work on now?"

"I'm going to go through each shell casing again and go over the clothing and belongings of Kylie Bowe once more. I'd hate to think that I missed something the first time around, but it's about all I have at the moment until we get something else to act on."

"All right," I said. "Let me know."

"Will do."

I reached out and hung the phone on the base. "Colt says the bullets are a match. The officer in Miami Gardens was killed with the same weapon used in Liberty City."

"Put a check mark by something we already knew," Steve said.

I shrugged. Movement outside my office window caught my eye. Garcia and Wade walked in.

"Ran into him on the elevator," Garcia said.

"Figured I'd just come up," Wade said. He held a couple of papers.

"What do you have?" I asked.

"We have no clue on where your video originated is what we have."

"Great," I said.

"It looks like it was emailed to each news outlet through a chained remailer service."

"What the hell is that?" Steve asked.

Wade ran his hand over his bald head. "Basically, when someone wants to send something anonymously, they can use a remailer. You send the message to a company, and they send it off to someone else anonymously. Yet that company still knows where the message came from. So, if that's where it started and ended, all we would have to do is find the company that sent the message, and they would be able to tell us where it came from. But that all goes to hell when you use a couple of the services. You send it to the one, they send it to another anonymously, they send it to another anonymously, and so on. Chained remailer basically means someone was smart enough to send this out without us being able to track down where it came from."

"So, we're screwed on that too," I said.

"Yeah," Wade said.

While he was delivering news that wasn't helping and that we sure as hell weren't looking for, something about the goofy look on his face said that he had something.

"Spill what you did find," I said.

"A coral rock fireplace," Wade said.

"What the hell is that?" I asked.

"Just what it sounds like. I thought the fireplace looked odd, so I did a little digging. The fireplace is made from coral rock."

"And that helps us how?" Steve asked.

Wade walked to my desk and set down a couple of papers. "These are stills from the video. Ever see a fireplace like this before?"

I glanced at the photos that had been printed. The rock of the fireplace was yellowed from age and smoke, I figured. It was obviously coral from its porous features. I'd never seen anything like it. "So how does this help us again?"

"The rarity," Wade said. "I started searching for coral rock fireplaces in Miami. Seems that this was in fashion in the nineteen twenties and thirties. We have a couple of things to go by here. The house this fireplace is in is going to be from that time frame. Now, even in that day, it wasn't something very common. Someone had money. People with money don't build small houses, and a little house probably wouldn't have lasted almost a hundred years. Basically, we're looking for a larger nineteen twenties or thirties home."

"Great, so how the hell do we find it?" I asked.

"Well, my search for homes for sale with coral rock fireplaces shows kind of a pattern as to where these homes are located." Wade moved around a couple of the photos he'd set on my desk until he had the one he searched for. He picked it up, looked at it for a moment, and handed it to me. "This is a map of houses for sale that hit on the search term 'coral rock.' See how they're all kind of in that area there?" Wade pointed at the map with the homes highlighted with little red and blue dots. Most of the properties were west of Highway 1 and coincidentally south of SW Twenty-Second Street, also known as Coral Way. "The red dots are homes for sale, and the blue dots are past sales. I'm thinking we start running patrols through these areas, looking for our BOLO vehicles," Wade said.

I nodded as I looked at the map. There was a definite pattern to the locations of the homes. I might have been looking at our best lead yet. "Nice work, Wade."

"Do you think we can get somewhere with it?" he asked.

I handed the printed map to Steve, who'd been leaning forward in his chair.

"Hopefully," I said. "Either way, it gives us something actionable. Good find."

"Thanks," he said.

After taking a quick look, Steve handed me the map.

"All right. Garcia, get some copies of that map and photos made up and shoot over to Halloway's office to show him this."

"Sure," Garcia said.

I reached for my phone. "Let me get the wheels turning to get some cars out in that area," I said.

CHAPTER 31

Clifford had spent the prior evening and morning preparing. He'd spent almost a hundred dollars on background checks from scammy looking websites. Most just stole his money, yet a couple delivered bits and pieces of information. Between the background checks and hours and hours of searching, Clifford had created a detailed profile on Sergeant Steve Walsh.

He'd learned the sergeant's age, his phone number and phone carrier, his address and how long he'd lived there, what station he worked at, and what kind of car he drove. Clifford learned that the cop was married to a woman named Sasha. The pair had no children. Clifford spent a little time getting some background information on the wife as well just in case it was needed.

After sending out the video, he'd filled a duffel bag with gear—guns, ammo, and his body armor. Clifford returned his rental car at the airport, went to the next rental car agency in line, and rented another. He wasn't certain that the cop he'd killed had reported the make and model that he'd been stopped in, yet Clifford wouldn't take a chance in case police were searching for it. The newer Nissan he'd just rented, a red full size, left a little to be desired. The car, only a year old, had shoddy body and paint work on the driver's side door. Accelerating caused the steering wheel to shake from what Clifford figured to be a bent wheel—he guessed it was probably from a woman who didn't know how to park and had hit a curb.

The interior of the car stank of stale cigarette smoke, the no-smoking stickers on the dash be damned. Clifford tried to put the condition of the vehicle out of his mind—he'd be in it for only a short time. He lifted the coffee to his lips and took a sip. The brew was good, a roast he'd never had before.

"Nice selection," he said, pleased with the choice he'd told the barista. Clifford lifted the small pound cake before him and took a bite. After his snack, he'd go find a spot for his reconnaissance.

The local news played on the television in the corner of the café. Clifford had seen his video play twice in the twenty minutes he'd been at the coffee shop. The news included a warning about graphic footage. It was only a matter of time before the cop saw it, if he hadn't already. Clifford imagined the police station was whipped into a frenzy. He wondered what the cop's reaction would be. Would he be angered, scared, worried? Clifford relished the thoughts of his threat worming around in the cop's head.

CHAPTER 32

It was twenty-five minutes. Twenty-five minutes from the point that I called for Patrol to search the area of town for the BOLO vehicles until we had the house. An officer spotted a big gray Land Rover parked in a carport of a 1920s home. The word was the large historic West Miami house was built entirely from coral rock. The officer ran the plate on the truck—it belonged to a man named Clifford Walton III. The address on the man was the West Miami home. The guy was forty-seven, white, five foot ten, and one hundred and eighty pounds—both of which qualified as average in my book. His sheet showed no priors.

Halloway wanted Walton's name spread through the Miami PD with a stop-and-detain order, but until we had confirmation on him being our guy, we'd keep his name from the press.

I put the orders out not to approach the house and to do whatever the hell they could to keep eyes on the place but not be spotted. Aside from door knocking the neighboring houses and asking the residents to vacate, I didn't want anything going down until we had SWAT in place. If this

Walton was our guy, we knew the man was armed, and the last thing that we wanted was a neighborhood shootout. I asked if there was a gold Chevy sedan on scene, and the report back was that there wasn't. The second we had our search warrant in hand, Steve and I left the station with Garcia and Ryan following us.

A sign reading West Miami Recreation Center and Park passed by on our left. I slowed and pulled behind a marked cruiser parked along the right side of the road. Another two cruisers were parked ahead of the patrol car sideways in the street. Steve and I exited the car. Garcia and Ryan had gone to meet with the officers stationed on the eastern side of the house. Five or six patrolmen were gathered at the vehicle blocking the road. One of the officers met Steve and me as we walked up.

"Sergeant Markle," he said. The officer, wide framed and dressed in Miami PD blues, looked to be somewhere in his forties. He had a round head with short black hair that formed a widow's peak.

"Lieutenant Harrington and Sergeant Walsh," I said. I pointed at Steve as I said his name.

"You're the guy this nut is after?" the sergeant asked, looking at Steve.

"I guess so," Steve said. "The house is where?"

"On the corner to our right up here. We have every street surrounding the home blocked off. All the neighboring houses have been vacated. There are officers on Southwest Nineteenth and Southwest Sixty-Second in case he tries fleeing on foot from the back of the home."

"All right," I said. "What's going on in the house? Any signs that he's inside?"

"We've got eyes on the place from those guys down there." Sergeant Markle pointed at the cars in the street past the roundabout and farther down the road where we stood. "No movement was the last report. We haven't seen anything that suggests there's anyone in the house. Every vehicle approaching our roadblocks is being checked then turned away in the opposite direction."

"Okay," I said.

"What are we doing here? Waiting on SWAT or what?"

"That's the plan. Should be within about ten minutes or so," I said. "I spoke with the SWAT lead a few minutes ago. They were loaded up and en route."

"Good," Markle said. "This is a fairly high traffic area, especially with the park. We're pissing off a lot of people by having this all shut down."

I nodded. "SWAT is going straight in. We don't want this guy to have any warning that we're outside. We know he's armed. We know that he has body armor. We're going to go in fast and try to use the element of surprise to our advantage."

"Basically, we don't want this asshole to get suited up inside his house and open fire on us and his neighborhood," Steve said.

"Understandable. What do you need from us?" Markle asked.

"Do we have everyone out of the neighboring houses?" I asked.

"Line of sight in each direction cleared."

"Then we need to hold down the fort until SWAT gets here," I said.

"Sure," Markle said. "Holler if you need anything." He said he was walking back to meet with his guys stationed at the blockade.

Steve had fished his phone from his pocket and had it to his ear. "Calling Ryan to see what he and Garcia see."

"All right," I said.

Steve said a few words to Ryan then passed me his phone.

"Yeah," I said as I brought the phone to my ear.

"Hey, we've got eyes on the front and southern side of this place," Ryan said. "The yard is fenced. I'm not sure if there is a back door or something on your side over there, but there isn't any exits other than windows on the southern side."

"Okay," I said.

"SWAT is coming in one of the armored trucks, right?" he asked.

"Bank truck," I said. The Miami PD had a couple of different special purpose vehicles—all had former commercial lives. Three of our SWAT trucks were repurposed armored vehicles that had seen previous time taking money back and forth across town. Another we called the dump truck, and aside from a box on the back, that was exactly what it was. Another had been an ambulance, yet another a delivery truck.

"Unless you, or they, think otherwise, I would say the front entrance here is probably the best bet for entry. Aside from the yard being fenced, the front perimeter along the sidewalk is fenced-in iron with a gate at the driveway. They can pull the truck right in, and it's going to block any chance of this guy leaving with a vehicle."

"All right. Let me call Petit and run it past him. I'm sure he already has the layout of the place etched into his head."

"You got it," Ryan said.

I handed Steve his phone and dialed Ethan Petit, the lead of our SWAT team. The phone rang in my ear.

"Yeah, Harrington. Three minutes," Petit said. His voice carried a heavy Cajun English accent. Petit was a late-thirties former Marine who had transferred in to Miami from somewhere in Louisiana a couple of years earlier.

"Okay. We have the area here locked down. PD blocking the street, the works. What's your entry point?"

"We're gonna knock on the front door with our door ram," Petit said. "See if anybody is home."

"So, you're going in the front," I said.

"Looks like the best way," Petit said. "Two minutes. We're going to come around past the park and get a look at the house before pulling up into the drive."

"You should be coming straight past us."

"You on Southwest Eighteenth?" he asked.

"Yeah."

"Then we'll see you soon."

"Okay. Let me go get everyone set."

"Mmm-hmm," Petit said. "We'll get in, get the place cleared, and I'll let you know when you can come on in."

"Perfect," I said and clicked off.

"Two minutes on SWAT," I called out. I stuffed my

phone back into my pocket. "They'll be coming right through here. Let's get these cars rolled apart so they can get through." I pointed at the two patrol cars blocking the street. An officer went to each one, and the cars moved from their positions. A moment later, a big black armored truck turned the corner and headed in our direction. The truck, painted a dull black with a gold stripe down the side, crept past. The word SWAT was just above the stripe and again written across the double back doors. At the roundabout, the truck made a right and disappeared. The cruisers that had moved then pulled back into the street and blocked the roadway. I waved for Steve to follow, and we drew our service weapons as we advanced up the block toward the house. I wanted a visual on the home and entry from our team.

As we neared the corner, I got my first good look at the home. Behind a waist-high fence surrounding the perimeter of the lot was the big brown-from-age colored-rock home.

The house looked out of place in its surroundings, as if it had been dropped in the center of town from a hundred years ago. The house was double the size of anything else in the neighborhood and resembled a prison or castle more than something residential. A big porch wrapped the front of the place. Each post supporting the roof over the porch was arched from one post to the next.

I spotted the SWAT truck clogging the home's driveway. In front of the truck, in the home's carport, was our big SUV. I could see the badges on the back of it. The fact that Charlotte Burrell, our red-haired prostitute, had actually fingered the correct vehicle was a bit of a shock.

"From the corner," Steve said. He pointed ahead of us at the cement pillar of the waist-high fence. At the corner of SW Eighteenth Street and SW Sixty-Second Street, we took up a covering position with aim on the front of the house. I saw Petit step from the passenger side of the truck. The rear doors opened, and four men dressed in full tactical gear emerged. Three had weapons drawn, and the fourth carried a door ram. The men grouped at the front of the truck. Petit gave Steve and me a quick glance and nod, and the men began to advance on the house. SWAT climbed the steps to the front patio and spread out to the sides of the front door. I had eyes on what I could see of the home's front windows, and I didn't see movement.

"Search warrant, Miami Police!" one of the men called.

I watched as the officer pounded the door ram through the home's big old double front doors, and the guys funneled into the house.

CHAPTER 33

A whistle and a wave from Petit, standing on the home's front porch, and Steve and I holstered our weapons. We passed through the open gate and walked the sidewalk toward the front door.

"No one home," Petit said. "This is your house, though."

Steve and I walked up the five steps to the redbrick front porch.

"What do you have inside?" I asked.

"A hell of a lot of dead animals and what looks like human hands in glass display cases."

"Show us," I said.

We followed Petit through the smashed-in front doorway. The interior of the home spread out before us. The entire floor was light-colored marble, just a shade or two off from the coloring of the walls. We'd entered the home into what I assumed was a large sitting room. I didn't spot a television anywhere. A glass coffee table sat on a big rug in the center of the room. Surrounding the table were a leather Chesterfield couch and a pair of chairs. Beyond the sitting area were a dining room and the kitchen farther off to the right. Petit waved over his shoulder for us to follow.

"I guess you could say his trophy room is back here," Petit said.

We continued into the home toward the kitchen and the hallway that ran alongside it. A pair of double doors leading into a big room stood open halfway down the hallway. Petit turned into the room.

"Damn," Steve said.

Describing the room that we'd entered as a trophy room was an understatement. I looked up and to my left and right. While the home appeared to be two stories from outside, the second story was only half of the upper level. To our backs, a loft overlooked us and the open area twenty feet above my head. Windows faced out in every direction above me. The walls were covered in animal mounts. I saw big cats, bear, deer, pigs, antelope, wolves, a cape buffalo, a rhino, even some animals I couldn't identify. He had the mounts of trophy animals from all over the world. A pair of recliners and a couch sat in front of an old looking wooden coffee table. A television sat on a small stand on the far end of the room. My eyes locked on the fireplace that Steve had already been walking toward. I walked to Steve's side. Petit followed.

Steve glanced over at me. "There are too many hands," he said.

My eyes went from one box to the next. We knew he took the hand of the prostitute, the man in Liberty City, and the officer. Yet Steve was right—I was looking at an extra one that we hadn't seen on video. "Let's get Colt in here. We're going to have to collect these and see what the hell they can tell us."

"Let me call him," Steve said.

"Tell him to bring Gomez or Harris or both of them," I said. "Aside from the house, we're going to have to deal with that truck as well. Get it towed back to the station or something."

"Sure," Steve said.

A couple of Petit's SWAT guys had joined us in the big room. Petit looked at one of his men. "Anything?" he asked.

"Gun room in the back," the guy said. "Or at least a room with a couple gun safes and some reloading equipment. I'm betting if we had showed when he was home, we would have had an entirely different situation here."

"Any weapons out?" I asked.

"Nothing that I saw," the officer said. "Aside from the gun room and this room, the lower level of the house isn't too interesting. A couple of spare bedrooms that don't look like they see much use. One is an office."

"Where's the master?" I asked.

"Guessing upstairs," the officer said. "Hamilton, Pecon, and Kilgo are up there."

"Hamilton," Petit called into his radio.

A second later, a "Yeah" came from above. One of the SWAT guys appeared at the iron railing of the loft.

"What do you have up there?" Petit asked, staring up at the man.

"Master bedroom and bath. Another big room with a pair of double doors that lead to the roof of the lower level."

"Anything of interest in the master?" I asked.

"It looked pretty much standard fare," the officer said.

"Some clothes and scattered shit lying around. Another gun safe in there."

"Okay. We'll get it all gone through," I said.

The officer gave me a nod and disappeared from the railing.

"Are you going to need anything else from us?" Petit asked. "Otherwise, we're going to head back in. Let these guys get back to work."

Most of the SWAT guys were trained patrolmen. They'd leave their beats when we needed their assistance but generally got back to their regular patrols as soon as whatever scene they were called to was under control.

"We're probably good," I said. "We've got Patrol on scene and the crime lab coming."

"Okay. I'll get the guys packed back into the sardine can." Petit stood there for a moment, looking around at all the animals. "Hell of a sight," he said. "Some of these are endangered and illegal as hell to have. I'm about a hundred percent certain that you shouldn't have the mount of what looks to be a black rhino." He pointed at the mount. "Or that," he said, pointing at a tiger. "Or whatever the hell that is," he said, pointing at a canine that looked almost hyena-like. "And then there's the mantel."

I nodded. "Yeah, the mantel with one more hand than we knew of."

Petit shook his head. "Good luck, Harrington," he said. "Catch him. Be safe about doing it."

"Thanks," I said. "I appreciate the help."

Petit motioned to his guys, and they left the room. I pulled out my phone and dialed the captain.

"Halloway," he answered.

"It's Harrington. The guy isn't here."

"Already in and cleared?" he asked. "Is it him?"

"Yeah. This is our guy all right. We need to start getting his name splashed everywhere."

"Okay. I'll get Mark on the line with whatever news outlets he can. We're going to get a photo of this shithead on the television about as soon as humanly possible. I'll get ahold of the airport and get the guy flagged."

"All right," I said.

"What's the house like?"

"Filled with the mounts of dead animals. That fireplace from the video is in what looks like an old ballroom. I'm standing in it now. You know, hold on a second," I said. Words weren't going to do justice to the room or what I was looking at. I snapped a pair of photos with my phone and sent them off to the captain's email. "Check your email," I said. "Me trying to describe it wasn't going to give you the full effect."

"Give me a second," the captain said.

I waited.

After hearing Halloway mumble a couple of choice profanities, I figured my photos went through.

"There's got to be hundreds of heads on the walls."

"Yeah," I said. "And an extra hand that we can't account for on the mantel."

The captain didn't respond. I got nothing but silence.

"Cap?" I asked.

"Yeah." He let out a big breath. "What do you need out there?"

"Steve was calling Colt and the crime lab. We're going to need them to collect the hands and deal with the SUV outside. I still need to go through this place and see what we have."

"All right. Let me get going on my end. Call me back if you find anything else. I'll start getting this guy's name distributed."

"Thanks, Cap."

"Yup," he said and clicked off.

I walked from the trophy room farther back into the house. I passed a bathroom, which was empty, and a home office. I popped into the office for a moment. A laptop computer sat on a desk. Framed hunting photos hung from the walls. At quick glance, I didn't see anything on the desk's surface that was of much interest. There was a small clock, a printer, some miscellaneous snail mail, and a cup of pens and pencils. I grabbed one of the pencils and used the tip to spread out a couple of envelopes. Two of the four letters were from a bank, another was from a phone carrier, and the last came from some wildlife foundation. The office would have to be gone through with a fine-toothed comb, and we'd need Wade or someone from Tech to address the computer. I left the office and continued to the end of the hall. A room went off to the right, a stairwell leading up to my left. I poked my head into the room and saw standing gun safes. I stepped inside.

Three standing gun safes took up the room's left wall. A big table with a reloading press sat along the back wall. Windows looked out to the side of the house that we had approached from and at the street out front. Steve was passing through the yard and toward the home's front door.

My eyes went to the walls of the room. As in the office, hunting photos were everywhere, showing a man, Walton, with various animals that he'd killed. Most included whatever weapon that he had killed the animal with. Pride covered his face in each image.

I went from one to the next, and most looked as if they were taken outside the US. One of the photos showed him and what looked like a jaguar. The background of the photo was tropical in nature—somewhere in Central or upper South America, I figured. The cat had a dart sticking out of it. I'd heard of darting hunting trips before. I'd also heard that they were just as frowned upon as killing whatever was being hunted in that manner. The tranquilizers used weren't very well regulated, and most of the time, the animals were overly sedated, having been shot multiple times. I shook my head and looked at the next photo. The picture was of Walton with a downed man wearing red paint. The man was dark skinned and wore not much more than a couple of scraps of cloth covering his midsection. A dart hung from the guy's collarbone area. The background was like that of the photo of the jaguar next to it. All I could think was that he went on a hunt and darted a human from some kind of previously uncontacted indigenous tribe in the jungle. I'd look into it further when time allowed.

My eyes went back to the gun safes. We were going to need a locksmith. Hopefully, the weapons involved in the case, or the body armor, were inside one of the standing safes or the one that was reported upstairs.

I turned to leave the gun room and search the second story of the house. Steve was walking down the home's hallway as I left the room and was about to head up.

"The crime lab is coming," Steve said. "What do you want to start with?"

"I'm going to take a peek in the master, then we can start going top to bottom, room to room." Garcia and Ryan were beyond Steve, standing near the kitchen at the hallway's end. I called back to them, "One of you guys let Sergeant Markle know he can open the roads back up."

"Sure," Garcia said.

He walked from the kitchen, and Ryan walked toward Steve and me. I turned and started upstairs. The guys followed.

CHAPTER 34

Parked outside the coffee shop, Clifford gripped the car's steering wheel with both hands. His knuckles were white. He pulled a hand from the wheel and grabbed his cup of coffee from the car's cup holder. His hand shook as he brought the drink to his lips. Clifford took a sip, spilling a bit of the beverage down his chin before setting the cup down. He swiped at the coffee on his face with the back of his hand.

Jerry, Clifford's neighbor, had called him a half hour before with the word that the police were sniffing around his house. Clifford couldn't comprehend why. When questioned further, Jerry told Clifford that they'd asked the neighborhood residents to leave their homes until further notice. Clifford was still on the line with his neighbor when Jerry said that a SWAT team was pulling into his driveway and armed men in tactical gear were entering his house. Upon hearing that information, Clifford smashed his phone in the middle of the coffee shop, generating wary looks and whispers from the hipsters sitting in a booth and the man and woman tapping away at their laptops.

Clifford rose from his chair and walked from the front of the coffee shop. He couldn't wrap his head around how the hell the cops had come looking for him. He hadn't been using his car. His prints weren't on record anywhere, nor was his DNA, not that they remotely had enough time to check into something like that. The video he emailed had bounced through three different remailers. Everything that he'd read online had assured him that method would be a hundred percent infallible. Clifford punched the dash of the rental car. With cops in his house, and in such force, it obviously meant they had his identity. They knew what he'd done.

"It had to have been the video," Clifford muttered. "Somehow." He shook his head. "I'm such an idiot."

The only point of filming and sending the video was to get the cop on guard—so the cop would be one hundred percent prepared when Clifford came calling. The thought of getting caught for it, or for any of his actions, had never even registered as a possibility. Yet there the police were, looking for him, and Clifford had no intentions of ever stepping foot into a prison.

He stared at the car's steering wheel and dug his fingers into his eyes. The cops would find out he'd rented the car the moment they had his banking records. He figured he had only a day, maybe just hours, until that happened. He couldn't go home, and he doubted he'd be able to get a flight. Clifford's only real option was to see how far he could get stealing people's cars, robbing people, and paying for everything in cash along the way. He figured if he could get up to the northwestern part of the US, he could buy the few things that he needed and disappear into the wilderness. Living off the land was an idea that intrigued him—he figured his survival skills were up to snuff.

Clifford's mind snapped from the thought as he brought the coffee to his lips for another sip. He'd used his debit card to buy the coffee and pound cake. If the cops were already on his bank account, they would see the charge.

"Shit," he said.

He started the rental car and pulled away from the front of the coffee shop.

CHAPTER 35

We'd been at the house for two hours. I'd been through every room of the home multiple times. I saw nothing that told us where this Clifford Walton III could be. The mail lying on his desk in the office gave us his phone number and carrier. We immediately tried to get a location on the phone but came up empty. We subpoenaed the carrier for records. From the pile of mail, we also got his banking information and account number. We were working on getting a real-time alert set up in case any charges came through and were waiting on the bank to get back to us with records.

Colt and the crime lab had been through every room. Each glass display box, complete with the skeletal remains of the hands, had been collected. Colt had full confidence in being able to match them up with the wounds on the bodies to see which came from which. Yet we still had a hand whose owner's identity we didn't know. Colt had said that he'd try to get a DNA sample from it.

Wade had taken Walton's laptop computer back to the tech center at our station. The laptop had facial and fingerprint recognition set up for security. Wade had said that it wasn't something that he could get through on location but should be able to without much of a problem back at the station. He said he'd let us know the moment he'd gained access to it.

"Anything?" Steve asked. He walked down the hall toward me.

I stood against the doorframe of the gun room, having watched Sean, the locksmith, work the lock for one of the standing safes. We frequently used the same company, and Sean, in his mid-fifties and a good hundred pounds overweight, was the owner. At that moment, he'd gone from drilling to hammering on the dial. The first one he'd gotten into was filled with hunting rifles.

I shook my head. "No pistols or body armor or hatchet yet," I said. "What did Halloway say?"

Steve had stepped outside to get an update on the things we were waiting on.

"We've got the banking records through yesterday."

"What about today?" I asked.

"I guess they don't get a batch report until after close of the business day or something. We won't have today's records until tomorrow."

"No real time?"

With my question, the whine of the power drill began again. I stepped farther into the hall so I could hear Steve talk.

"They have an alert set up for it now," Steve said. "Basically, anything that has happened this morning, we won't have a record of until tomorrow, but as of now, anything new that comes in, we'll know about."

"All right," I said. "Anything of interest over the last couple days?"

"Yeah. A rental car from the airport."

"What kind? Plate number?"

"Halloway called and dug into it just before I called him. Turns out it was a gold Chevy sedan. Returned this morning."

"So, it was our car?"

"Looks that way. I sent Garcia and Ryan over there to see what they could get from the airport security cams. They just left."

"If he dropped off a car, he had to have left somehow," I said. "Do we know he didn't get on a plane?"

"No flight out," Steve said.

"All right. So maybe he took a cab or shuttle somewhere. If we can get him on video leaving, maybe we can get a location from whoever was driving him."

Steve nodded and jerked his chin back at the gun room. I hadn't even noticed the whine from the drill had stopped. I spun back around the corner to have a look. Sean, the locksmith from Lock and Key Specialties, yanked at the handle of the door, and it swung open.

"Let's see what's behind door number two," Sean said. He wiped some sweat from his forehead with the back of his forearm.

Steve and I walked into the room so we could get a look. The standing safe was the largest in the room and, from what Sean had said, would take the longest to get into. The interior of the safe was separated into sections. Two big rectangles for standing rifles took up the left and right sides of the interior. Both sides were filled with shotguns. At a quick glance, it looked like a dozen. Running directly up the middle were random-sized shelves filled with boxes of shells, ammunition boxes, and cleaning equipment. The top shelf, which spanned the entire safe, was filled with paperwork and file folders. A passport and a stack of ten thousand dollars in hundreds sat off to the right. The back of the safe door held pistols in holsters, four across and four down. A couple of storage pouches sat below the holsters.

"Looks like we found our handguns," Steve said. "Hopefully we can make a connection."

"Hopefully," I said. "Though I can't say that that isn't a little concerning." I held out two fingers at the two empty pistol holsters at the top of the safe door. The names of the weapons were printed on pieces of tape stuck to each holster. I imagined it was to identify which weapon went where—the holsters mostly concealed the weapons themselves. Both empty holsters had the word "Springfield" written on the pieces of tape stuck to them. "Every inch of the safe is used, and we have two voids. Guessing by the little labels here, they were probably Springfield pistols."

"So where are the two missing guns?" Steve asked.

I motioned for the locksmith to start on the next safe while Steve and I had a better look at the paperwork and contents of the top shelf. I reached for the passport with my gloved hand and started going through it. The book was mostly full, as our Clifford Walton was quite the traveler. Steve had grabbed a stack of papers and was paging through them.

"What do you have?" I asked.

"Nothing. This all looks like travel information. Flight itineraries, hotel bookings, some receipts for stays at lodges. Stuff like that. A lot of this looks like it's from out of country." Steve held a sheet out toward me. "Read Spanish?"

"Enough to order off a menu," I said. "We're going to need to get all the paperwork pulled out and boxed up. These weapons are all going to have to go as well."

"Let me get Colt," Steve said. "We'll need a couple totes, plus he's going to probably want to photograph all of this and catalog all of the firearms before pulling them."

"Sure," I said. Steve walked from the room.

"This one should only take me a second," Sean said. "Not quite on the quality level with the other two."

"All right," I said.

Sean got to work, drilling holes in the combination dial, sticking a screwdriver in one, and a moment later popping the dial off. He drilled and hammered for another minute or two, and just as Steve and Colt were walking into the room, Sean yanked the door open.

"More rifles, more ammo, more of the same," Sean said.

I got my look, but aside from the long guns, there was nothing of interest.

"Any paperwork?" Steve asked.

"Zip," I said. "Just the firearms."

The sound of a photo being snapped came from Colt a few feet away. He'd started getting his pics of the first safe and the weapons inside. "This guy had quite the arsenal," Colt said. "Nice rifles as well. It looks like he has a couple Kimber and

Weatherby rifles in here." Colt snapped more pics. "Some of these guns are almost two grand a pop. There's probably ten thousand dollars' worth of rifles in here."

"The shotguns and handguns are easily that much or more," Steve said. "Nice shotguns aren't cheap, and he's got a bunch."

"Look at the photos in here and that trophy room. Guns and hunting were this guy's life. Obviously, he had the means. That truck outside costs a small fortune, and this house doesn't exactly strike me as cheap, either."

"No, it doesn't," Steve said.

"You said there was another safe somewhere upstairs?" Sean asked. He loaded his tools back into the box he'd brought into the house.

"In the master bedroom," I said. "Smaller, like a document fire safe."

"Did you want to point me in the right direction?" Sean asked.

"Um, yeah. Are you guys good here?" I asked.

"We got it," Steve said.

I nodded, told Sean to follow, and left the room. I walked up the steps to the second floor. Behind me, Sean was huffing and puffing. The tools inside his box clanked as he bounced the box off his leg with each step up. I stopped at the top of the steps and looked back at him. He'd made it only about halfway up. He'd set the tools down and was taking a breather. He didn't seem old enough or out of shape enough for the stairs to be that much of a problem.

"Need a hand?" I asked.

"Nah. I'm just old, fat, and have bad knees and ankles. No cartilage at all in my left of each. That's why I own a ranch," Sean said.

"Want me to try to carry the safe downstairs?" I asked.

"Well, shit. If I would have known that was an option, I would have sat my big ass on the couch and had you bring it to me." Sean cracked a smile. "Nah. This will be my painful exercise for the month. Maybe I'll take the doc up on those cortisone shots he's been telling me to get." Sean scooped up his toolbox by the handle and climbed the rest of the steps one at a time while using the handrail for leverage.

We got to the master, and he made short work of the safe. Inside were more documents, most of which looked related to the home. Some were from the will that we figured had belonged to Clifford Walton's father, judging by the name on the sheets. We'd have to go through each item.

"Thanks for the help, Sean," I said.

He gave me a nod as he loaded up his tools.

CHAPTER 36

"We have Clifford Walton on video returning one rental car and getting another," Garcia said.

"When?" I asked.

I stood in the conference room of the homicide bureau. Papers that we'd pulled from Walton's home covered the entire long table. Lieutenant Lopez offered to interpret the papers that were written in Spanish. Some appeared to be in Russian as well. We were waiting on someone to come in and help us with those. Our previous go-to guy on anything Russian turned out to be organized crime. He was currently spending time behind bars and wasn't going to be much help.

"He rented the new one right after returning the other one," Garcia said. "Early this morning, around eight thirty or so."

"From the same place at the airport?"

"Airport, yes. But a different rental car company a couple doors down. Returned the one, walked to the next rental office, and filled out the paperwork for another vehicle."

"What did he rent?" I asked.

"They put him out in a burgundy 2016 Nissan Altima. I

put the tag number out across the wire already. Unfortunately, they don't have a way to track their vehicles."

"Damn," I said.

"First thing I asked," Garcia said. "We've got a pretty good look at him on video, though. Seems he's bald-headed now. Basically, the hair on the sides and back of his head in the photo we have up on the news is gone. I already put that information out there."

"All right. Can we get a copy of the video?" I asked.

"Wade was my next call," Garcia said.

"Okay. Let's see what we can do there. Tell Wade to call me when he gets off the phone with you. I want to see how he's coming with that computer."

"Sure," Garcia said. "Did you guys get anything?"

"Not really. We're in the conference room, sorting out all the paperwork we retrieved from the house. We're going to go through it and start making some phone calls. See if we can find anything."

"Does he have any family in the area?" Garcia asked.

"Cap said he couldn't find anything," I said. "Single, never married, parents deceased."

"Friends?"

"We don't know," I said.

"Okay. Let me call Wade. I'll let him know to call you."

"Sounds good," I said.

"See you when we get back."

"All right," I said and clicked off.

"What was that?" Steve asked.

"Ryan and Garcia found some video of the guy at the

airport. He returned one rental car and got another from a different rental car company at the airport. The make, model, and tag, Garcia already distributed."

"Why is he renting rental cars?" Lopez asked.

Lieutenant Mateo Lopez, husky and mid-forties, held the same position that I did but covered the southern part of the greater Miami area. He scratched at his short black spiked hair and appeared to be awaiting my response.

"Don't know," I said. "But an educated guess is so that no one sees him doing anything illegal in his big-ass Land Rover that sticks out like a sore thumb."

"He took it a step further with pulling the tag from the last rental car and putting a stolen tag on it," Steve said. "Which makes me think that he could do that very same thing again. The BOLO should be on the make and model of the rental vehicle. Screw the tag."

Steve had a good point. I pulled out my phone to call Patrol, but it rang before I could dial—Wade. "Call Patrol," I said to Steve. "I have Wade calling me now."

He nodded.

I clicked Talk. "Yeah, Wade," I said.

"Your guy was searching Walsh on this computer," Wade said. "Looking for whatever information he could find."

"That's what you got from it?" I asked.

"Yeah. It looks like a bunch of background check places and random internet searches. What he actually got from any of it, I can't tell, but he was definitely sniffing around."

I let out a big breath. "All right," I said. "Garcia called you about the video?"

"He did. I'm sending someone out to him while I keep digging through this computer," Wade said.

"Okay. Let me know what else you get."

"You got it." I clicked off from my call and waited for Steve to finish his with Patrol.

"They have the BOLO on the car," Steve said. He stuffed his phone back into his pocket. "That was Wade?"

"Yeah. He says the computer shows that this Walton was searching for information on you."

"What kind of information?" Steve asked.

"Background checks and miscellaneous internet searches. He says he can't tell if the guy actually got anything."

"What the hell is he going to get? My name and number are in the phone book. Same with my address. My photo and bio are up on the station's website. Unless he's planning on finding my social to steal my identity…" Steve held up his hands, as if in question.

"The point is he was looking into you. The threat he made is probably pretty credible," I said.

"To hell with whoever this asshole is and his threats. Come after me. I hope he does." Steve patted his shoulder-holstered firearm. "He better be in his little armor outfit."

"Pump the brakes, Shooter," I said.

Steve gave me the side-eye.

"Listen. All accounts show that he's familiar, probably highly skilled, with firearms," I said. "He's shown that he will attack unprovoked. Let's try to use brains instead of brawn."

Steve grumbled something that I couldn't make out. My guess was more tough talk. We continued sorting and going over the recovered papers. In total, we had what we could confidently say was twelve trips taken to different countries. We had flight information to go along with the booked hunting trips and lodging.

We started dialing, coming up empty time and time again. It seemed that Walton had gone solo on each hunting trip and had nothing planned with the same companies in the immediate future. Officer Alex Ivanovich came in and looked over the paperwork we believed to be Russian. He said it was Ukrainian, but he was still familiar and made some phone calls for us, anyway. Again, we came up empty. By a couple of minutes after six o'clock, we'd been through every paper and weren't any closer to finding someone he'd traveled with, someone he'd known personally, or finding out where he'd be in the future. I thanked Lieutenant Lopez and Officer Ivanovich for giving us a hand and got all the paperwork organized into a file box.

"Now what?" Steve asked.

I pushed the box across the conference table toward him. "Take that down to Evidence to be booked in with the other stuff from the house. I'm going to check in with Colt and Wade then get everyone in here for a quick meeting. Ten minutes, max. Just a refresher of everything we got for the day, bring Dave and his guys up to speed, then we'll take off. Amy sent me a text a couple minutes ago. She and Sasha want to order in some Chinese."

"Okay," Steve said.

As he walked out of the conference room with the file box, I caught Garcia and Ryan walking toward their desks in the bull pen. I waved them over.

"What's shaking?" Garcia asked as he walked through the conference room door.

"Did you guys just get back?" I asked.

"We just walked in," Ryan said. "Tech has the video. What did we miss?"

"Us sorting paperwork and running up the station's long-distance bill."

"Anything?" Ryan asked.

I shook my head. "No. He wasn't booked for anything upcoming, and aside from him being a customer, no one really seemed to know him personally."

"We don't have any clue where this guy could be going?" Garcia asked. "Is he running, is he in the area, does he have someone hiding him out or helping him?"

"We have his ID everywhere. I'd like to get Mark from the PR department to put together a new media package on this guy. Just adding bits and pieces isn't working for me. I want the press to have his face, name, the fact that he now has his head shaved, and the vehicle we believe him to be driving."

"Do you want me to go find Mark?" Garcia asked.

"Yeah. Ryan, why don't you run downstairs quick and round up Colt and Wade. I'll get the cap and Dave. Steve just went to drop a file box off in Evidence, so he'll be back up in a second. As soon as we're all here, we'll start. This is going to be short and sweet, basically just bringing the night shift up to speed, getting everyone on the same page, and making sure Mark has what he needs to get something complete out to the media."

CHAPTER 37

Sometime between waiting for the perfect mark and leaving the airport's long-term lot in the woman's minivan, he'd made the decision. He was on the run. When the police caught him—that was, if they ever did—one or two more bodies weren't going to make a bit of difference. He'd called out the cop for a reason, and now, the stakes couldn't be higher. The cop couldn't be more ready. Killing the cop, taking his trophy, and getting away was the ultimate challenge. The ultimate hunt.

Clifford sat in the police station parking lot, staring out of the windshield of the woman's minivan from the second row of seats. He'd hoped the tinted windows were enough to block anyone outside from seeing him inside, yet he'd still been ducking out of sight when he saw anyone. Clifford knew the cop's car. The motor vehicle records he'd pulled showed a mid-eighties Buick was registered to him. Clifford found the Buick, which turned out to be a jet-black Grand National.

The Grand National was parked in the lot between a rusted seventies Ford Bronco and a grass median. As Clifford watched the GN, he almost felt bad about what he planned to do. Clifford had always had an affection for cars, and the Grand National the sergeant drove was the baddest American car on the streets in the 1980s. Clifford wondered what the cop had done to it under the hood. Another thought bubbled up. His attack would have to come as a surprise and would need to be flawless—he wouldn't be catching up to the sergeant or outrunning the man's car in the woman's stolen minivan.

Clifford looked at his watch. The time was after six. "What the hell time does this cop work until?" He took his eyes from the vehicle and stared past it at the police station's back door.

CHAPTER 38

Our meeting ended up taking longer than I'd expected. Colt came to the meeting with a new find. He'd recovered blond hairs from the back of the Land Rover, which had been flat-bedded to the garages in our station. He said he'd have to get a sample of Kylie Bowe's hair from Skip to check it against to see if it belonged to her or someone else. Colt said he was going to stay late until he had that information.

Wade didn't have a ton to add to the meeting—he hadn't found anything new on Walton's computer aside from hunting photos and videos. His plan was to go through all of them in detail the next morning.

We gave Mark what he needed to put together something for the press. He said he'd get everything out to the media outlets in time for the nightly news.

Dave and the overnight guys who joined the meeting had been brought up to speed. There wasn't much for the night shift to act on. I imagined the bulk of their shift would be spent working the phones and fielding phone calls that came through the tip line. Dave said he'd give me a ring if anything of merit came through.

Steve followed me from the back door of the station.

"Did they still want to do Chinese?" Steve asked.

"Yeah, Amy sent me about a hundred text messages while we were in the meeting. Apparently, they're starving and have flies buzzing around them. Her last text said they didn't have much time left. I just told her to put in an order."

"What did they get me?" Steve asked.

"I don't know. Chinese food," I said.

Steve waved his hand, dismissing the topic. "I'm sure Sasha got me something edible. She's usually pretty good with remembering what I like. They know we're going to be a bit, right?"

"Yeah," I said. "I told her we had to run to your house before we get there."

"Okay," Steve said. "I'll try to make it quick." He walked to the door of his car and stuck the key into the lock. "Thankfully Sasha sent me a detailed list of all the shit she needs me to bring to her. Any clue what a contour brush is?"

"None," I said.

"That makes two of us," Steve said. "I'm just going to sweep all of her stuff off the top of the bathroom vanity into a bag and hope for the best."

"Good luck with that," I said. I pulled open the Bronco door and hopped inside. "Lead the way."

Steve got into his car and fired the motor. I followed him from the lot and made a left out onto NW Twenty-Fifth street that ran past the front of our building. We took NW Twenty-Fifth until we made a right on NW 107th a mile or so down. We traveled north about three miles, passing the westernmost side of the president's golf club and resort along the way. The neighborhood quickly turned to country.

Steve made a left on the main road that led into his subdivision. Nothing but palm trees took up the left and right of the street. Beyond were fields. I waited for an oncoming car to pass so I could make the turn. As I waited and the oncoming car neared, a minivan coming from behind passed me in the oncoming lane, shot through the intersection, and made the left turn after Steve. If I'd had lights and sirens on the Bronco, I would have had them on and pulled the driver over. Turning left behind a vehicle waiting to turn left wasn't exactly legal. I waited for the oncoming car to pass and got stuck waiting for another one that was perfectly timed to prevent me from going. The second car passed, and I made the corner. I could see both the back of the minivan and Steve's car ahead of me. The minivan was once more in the oncoming lane. I assumed it was trying to pass Steve—again, something that would have been illegal on that specific road. I continued to watch as the van shot to the right and Steve's car began to spin.

It took me a moment to get a grip on what I'd just seen. "He hit him," I said.

The two cars appeared to be stopped in the street a good quarter mile ahead. I kept my foot on the gas, but the Bronco was going to get there when it got there—going fast was not one of its strong suits. I was nearing, still a good eighth mile away, when I saw the driver's door of the minivan swing open. I got closer. The driver had on a mask—all black. He was holding a pair of pistols, one in each hand. He rounded the back of his minivan and opened up on Steve's Grand National just as I was coming to a stop in the street. The second I did, he turned the guns on me.

"Shit," I said and immediately slammed my body down across the cab of the truck. The sound of gunfire filled my ears. One shot after another. I could hear and feel the rounds ripping through the front of my truck. I saw a couple of holes punch through the floorboards from the bullets penetrating. The windshield splintered and tossed shards of glass at me. I pulled at my service weapon in the holster under my jacket. The instant I heard a break in the gunfire, I rose and tried to get my aim. I couldn't see the shooter. I yanked the door handle, put my feet on the street, and used the door for cover as I again looked for the shooter. The minivan blocked my view of all but the back of Steve's car. I didn't see Steve anywhere.

"Steve!" I shouted. I left the cover of the Bronco and made my way to the back of the minivan. I quickly poked my head around the side. I saw the back of our shooter with Steve still behind the wheel of his car. The entire driver's side of the Grand National was littered with bullet holes. Movement from our shooter caught my eye. I saw a hatchet blade rise up into the sky above the shooter's right shoulder. "Drop it!" I shouted.

He didn't even look at me.

"Walton! Drop the weapon!"

His body flexed—he was about to deliver the blow. The instant the blade inched downward, I fired three times into his back. Walton's body jerked, and he dropped the hatchet. In a flash, he spun around and fired. I ducked behind the minivan for cover. By the time I spun around the corner of the van and tried to get a shot, he was gone from view. A split second later, I heard a door slam and the van's motor wail. I took three steps away from the van as it rocketed forward, spinning tires down the street. I fired through the side and back windows. The van's front right tire spewed smoke as it fought for traction. I put another couple of rounds into the vehicle as it sped off. The motor screamed, and he kept getting farther away. Gunfire came from Steve at his car. He sent a few rounds in the direction of the van and collapsed to the ground beside his driver's door.

"Son of a bitch!" I shouted. I holstered my weapon and jogged to Steve. I immediately saw blood everywhere. Blood was all over the inside of his car and all over him and the ground beneath. A big gash hung open across his forehead. Steve's left hand held his leg, and his right held his weapon. "Where are you hit?" I asked.

"A couple times in the left leg," Steve said. "I'm leaking pretty good."

"Your head?" I asked.

"He was on me before I even knew what the hell happened. The second I reached for my gun, he hit me in the face with the butt of the hatchet."

"Get your belt around your leg," I said. I yanked my phone from my pocket and began dialing 9-1-1.

"Go after him," Steve said.

"I'm not leaving you."

Steve lifted his chin at a couple of oncoming cars. "Someone will help. Go."

"The Bronco isn't going to catch shit."

"Take my car and get the hell after him!" Steve did his best to get away from the driver's door. "Go!"

I jammed my phone back into my pocket, jumped behind the wheel of his car, and slammed the door closed. Shattered safety glass from the windows flew across the car and sloshed back and forth inside the driver's side door. I yanked the car into Drive and thumped the gas. The tires went up in a cloud of smoke. When they caught, I launched forward. Steve on the ground and my Bronco in the street became small in the rearview mirror. Wind whipped through the shot-out windows. I glanced at the car's speedometer which was pegged to the right of eighty-five miles per hour, the highest the analog gauge read. I looked forward. Two cars came in my direction. I couldn't see the minivan ahead. Steve's road blurred past outside my driver's side window void.

I'd been around the outskirts of Steve's neighborhood a couple of times. The road that I was on came to an end, and I could only go left. The road that went left was bordered entirely on the western side by a sound wall that ran along Florida's Turnpike. Aside from the wall, it dead-ended and had only two connecting roads that both were gated and both led back into Steve's subdivision—none of which were facts that I figured the shooter, presumably Walton, knew.

I sped toward the turn, locked up the brakes, and slid around the corner, almost taking out the sign that read Ninetieth Street. The moment I was pointed south, I locked eyes on the minivan a quarter mile ahead and floored the gas.

I ripped my phone from my pocket and dialed Halloway.

"What's up, Harrington?" he answered. "What the hell is that noise?"

"Wind. I'm chasing down Walton. He just shot Steve. Make sure he has paramedics coming." I was reeling the minivan in. The quarter mile quickly became an eighth. Walton didn't have a chance of outrunning Steve's car.

"What? Where the hell are you?" Halloway asked.

"In his neighborhood. I'm on Ninetieth Street. Get some cars out here. Walton is in a black minivan, missing windows." The van got closer and closer. Just a few car lengths separated us.

"Plate?" the captain asked.

I slammed the nose of Steve's car into the back of the van. The rear tires of the minivan lifted into the air from my front bumper getting under the rear bumper of the van. I slammed on the brakes, and the minivan swerved as it freed from my front bumper. Walton floored the gas to flee. I did the same and again was on the van's rear bumper.

The captain's voice echoing from the speaker in my phone faded into the background. I saw a dead-end sign shoot past out the passenger side of the car. I looked down at our speed. Forty something. I hit the gas, got my front fender even with the minivan's rear left wheel, and yanked my steering wheel to the right. The front of Steve's car crushed into the minivan's quarter panel and sent it sideways. The van swerved, snapped back in the other direction, and left its wheels. It crashed down onto its side, briefly showing its undercarriage before its momentum lifted it again. Shattered glass and broken shards of plastic flew from the vehicle. The minivan made a single revolution, spinning as it did, and righted itself. The nose of the van pointed directly at me. It rocked back and forth, almost tipping onto its side, before coming to rest in a cloud of dust and debris.

I locked up the brakes and slid to a stop. Movement from the driver caught my eye. I snatched my service weapon from my shoulder holster and stepped from the car.

CHAPTER 39

The van was twenty yards from me. Fluids leaked from underneath it and were puddling on the ground. Leaking aside, the motor still ran. The windshield of the minivan was shattered, splintered, and pulled from the framework at the top corner of the crushed roof. Through the windshield's void, I saw the driver adjust the black mask covering his face. Dust and smoke from the airbags hung in the air around the man, presumably Walton, moving inside.

"Kill the engine! Hands out the window!" I shouted. I used the driver's door of Steve's car for cover and aimed my weapon at the man inside the van. The motor didn't shut down. Hands didn't appear out of the window as I'd instructed. The person inside the van was moving violently, as if they were yanking at something. What, I couldn't tell.

"Shut the vehicle off. Throw the keys out the window. Put your hands where I can see them. Now!" I shouted.

The violent actions of the person inside continued. None of my orders were followed. All I could see of the person was half of a black mask. I heard a clunk of the transmission, and the front tires of the minivan smoked. He was trying to flee.

I fired everything left in my gun straight into the oncoming van. The motor's pitch didn't change, and it didn't slow.

I was wrong that it was someone trying to flee. The minivan didn't take the open lane to get past the Grand National—it came straight for me, tucked in behind the driver's door of the car. I'd be crushed with a direct hit. My mind must have subconsciously worked out my options for fleeing because I didn't have time to assess the situation.

I planted my left foot and dove away from the side of the car. My eyes never came from the nose of the minivan bearing down on me. As I flew through the air, I saw the van make contact with the front fender of Steve's car. I heard the impact and crunching metal. I saw the nose of the van impact the door. Even while seeing daylight on the far side of the van, I knew I was going to be hit before I reached the ground.

In a fraction of a second, every possibility of injury flashed through my head—from getting hit full on, run over, and lying in the street dying to having my pelvis crushed and being paralyzed. The thought of my legs being mangled and taken from me was followed by the thought of spending life in a wheelchair. I closed my eyes and waited. I felt the impact, directly to the side of my right shoe. I remember the feeling of spinning through the air and the crack of my face and chest against the roadway. The sound of scraping metal quickly turned into the sound of tires sliding.

I opened my eyes. I saw sand-covered blacktop. I tried wiggling my toes—they all wiggled, albeit a bit too freely. I could feel my shoes were gone. I went for a knee bend on the right side then the left—both worked. I turned my head and saw Steve's GN with the driver's door hanging down and touching the street. With the back of my hand, I brushed at my right eyebrow. My hand came back wet with blood. As I looked at it, the realization dawned that my gun wasn't in my hand.

"Hey," I heard.

Tactical looking boots entered my field of view.

I coughed and rolled onto my side. The man stood over me with a pair of pistols pointed straight down at my face. I got a good look at the guy behind the guns. Aside from his ballistic mask, which was down, he wore full body armor. His legs were covered with ballistic drop leg platforms—basically armor for the hips, thighs, and femoral arteries. More armor hung lower, covering his knees. It looked custom, possibly homemade. The vest he wore also appeared to have some added plating for his shoulders.

"Where's your gun?" he asked.

I didn't know and didn't respond. I looked past the guy up the street toward the direction where help would be coming from. I saw no flashing lights and heard no sirens.

"Have a backup?" he asked.

Again I didn't respond. Our department prohibited backup firearms. While most officers would have liked the option to carry them, and backups had been proven to save officers' lives time and time again, the uninformed public thought they could be used to plant evidence in police shootings that ended up being questionable. It wasn't a possibility. The weapon still had to be registered with the department as being carried in the field. As it was, I didn't have one. I let out a breath and rolled to get my knees beneath me. Unarmed or not, I wasn't going to sit there and let the guy kill me. If there was a chance I could do anything to save myself and take him out, I was damn well going to attempt it.

I got on all fours. A stream of blood leaked from my face and started forming a puddle beneath me. I felt a kick to my side that sent me flat onto my back. I stared at the sky. My body jerked, trying to breathe. A cough came, and I filled my lungs with air. I coughed again, pulled in another breath, and rolled onto my side to get up for the second time.

"Oh, I think we have something here," he said.

I didn't know what the hell he was talking about and didn't much care. I got a knee beneath myself and pushed off to stand. I immediately felt a shooting pain through my right foot. I tried putting a bit of weight on it. Something was broken. The pain coming from my foot was going to have to wait. I locked eyes on the man.

"You're a fighter, eh?" he asked. His voice sounded muffled beneath his mask.

I swayed a bit and got as stable of a stance as I could get on a bum wheel.

He kept one gun pointed at me and holstered his other one on the front of his body armor. He lifted the mask from his face and pulled it off. Blood covered his forehead and ran down his cheek. More blood ran down the left side of his bald head. He dropped the mask in the street.

"Clifford Walton," I said.

"Yes, sir," he replied. "Who are you?"

"Lieutenant Harrington. Miami Homicide. You're under arrest."

He laughed and unfastened a belt that was securing his leg armor. He let it drop to the ground then took a step forward to remove his feet from the armor. Walton kicked it to the side.

My eyes scanned left and right across the pavement. I didn't see my service weapon anywhere, though I did see my shoes. One was about ten feet away in the middle of the street. Another was on the complete opposite side of the road. How the hell it could have possibly gotten there, I didn't know. My eyes went back to Walton. He pulled out the weapon that he'd just holstered.

"Do you have a backup firearm?" he asked.

I said nothing. My mind was filled with the logistics of how to get to him. He was fifteen feet away, and I was shoeless on a bad foot. I couldn't come up with anything that was going to get me to him before getting shot.

He brought both weapons up and pointed them at my face.

"I'm going to ask you again," he said, "and if you don't answer me, I'm firing. Do you have a backup firearm?"

"No," I said.

"Lift your pant legs. One at a time."

I did as he asked, lifting my right pant leg then my left. Anything to keep him exactly where he was and buy some additional time for backup to arrive.

"Your suit jacket. Take it off and toss it," Walton said.

I pulled my jacket off and tossed it a few feet off to my right.

"Let me see your waist, front and back," he ordered.

I stared past him, hoping a patrol car would come into view. I saw nothing but a half mile of empty road.

I pulled my shirt from where it was tucked in and lifted the front. As I turned around to show him that I didn't have a weapon tucked into my rear waistline, I pulled my extra magazine from my shoulder holster. Wherever my weapon was, I knew it was empty. I dumped the magazine into my front pocket and turned back toward him. I let my shirt drop from my hands.

"The holster. Take it off and toss it."

"There's nothing in it," I said. *Anymore*, I thought.

"Do it."

I pulled my holster off and tossed it to the side of the road.

"Empty your pockets. Take off your belt with your cuffs and everything else."

"What the hell are you doing? What's the point?" I asked.

"Do it or I'm taking that right knee from you," Walton said. "Just like I did to that other cop."

I saw him drop his aim. I assumed the other cop he was referencing was the Miami Gardens PD Officer he'd killed, Pazanis.

I pulled off my belt and tossed it along with the little utility pouch that held my cuffs.

"Satisfied?" I asked.

"Pockets," he said.

I hoped he had forgotten about that part—he hadn't. I jammed both hands into my pockets and pulled my phone from the one and wallet from the other. I tossed them both into the street. The gun magazine remained in my right pocket. I reached into both and pulled out what I could of the linings—mostly just the left side. I gave them a pat to insinuate they were empty. "I don't have anything on me," I said.

"Good," Walton said.

It seemed that he bought what I sold. He dropped the magazine from one pistol then racked the slide and ejected a bullet. He slid the magazine into a pouch on his vest and holstered the weapon. He did the same with the other gun. Walton tightened the Velcro strap holding down the weapon in the holster and raised his hands. He balled both into fists. "Let's go," he said.

He started advancing.

I was trying to wrap my head around what the hell I was looking at. Walton, a bit smaller than I, had disarmed himself and apparently was looking for a fistfight. I'd oblige.

I brought my fists up and did my best to solidify my fighting stance. I dropped my hands immediately when I realized his intentions. With both my hands blocking his foot and me pulling my right leg up to block the kick, he still connected with enough force to drop me to a knee. He kicked me in my manhood with his tactical boots, and I imagined every bit of power he had. The second my knee hit the ground, he swung a right to my eye. My head dipped down from the punch only to be lifted by a knee to my chin.

I shook my head.

"I'm going to beat you to death," he said.

Walton had taken a couple of steps back. He bounced on

his toes left and right like a fighter in a ring. He came in again as I was getting back to my feet. I brought my hands up for a block of what I figured was going to be a punch but was ready if he went for another low blow. Walton did a pirouetting spin kick. His foot came at my ear, and I got enough of an arm up to get a block. Before I could swing on him, he delivered a pair of knee strikes to my left ribs and retreated a couple of feet away. Standing in front of Steve's car again, Walton bounced from his left foot to his right.

He'd obviously had martial arts training, and I had no intentions of standing there and being his punching—or in that case, kicking—bag. He came lunging at me again, but I was ready. I planted my left foot and launched myself toward him, going for a shoulder tackle. My actions must have caught him by surprise because he squared himself toward me and gave me a perfect tackling dummy.

The second step that I took off my right foot left a little to be desired, but I wrapped my arms around him the moment I made contact. I put all the power I had into driving him back into the side of Steve's car. We hit hard enough to cave in the quarter panel. The side window of the car had already been blown out, leaving nothing but shards of safety glass in the frame—safety glass that did its best to skin the meat from my arm. I let him go and delivered an uppercut to his chin. His head snapped back. I put an elbow into his left eyebrow, which instantly opened a two-inch-wide gash. I put another strike to the exact same area. As I was going for the third, he blindly shoved me backward. I advanced, only to get low blowed by an unexpected kick again. A looping left fist that I barely saw sent me to the ground. I felt a blow square to my back that put me flat. It had to have been a stomp.

My head faced Steve's car. I had a clear view beneath it. My eyes locked on my gun, under the car near the front tire on my side. I rolled onto my back as Walton was going for another stomp. His foot, lifted high, came down at my chest. I moved to the side just in time. He whiffed with his stomp, hitting nothing but street. The moment his boot came down, I grabbed it and twisted. A forearm to the back of his knee completed the takedown. Walton dropped to his knees on the street. I rolled toward him and brought him the rest of the way down. The moment he was in my control, I slammed his face into the street and dove toward Steve's front tire.

My hand found the grip of my gun. I snatched it and got myself to a seated position against Steve's front tire. I needed to get eyes back on Walton. He'd already gotten himself on all fours. I dropped the magazine that I knew was empty from my gun and fumbled at my pocket for the one I'd gotten from my holster before throwing it. I watched Walton get to his feet. He turned toward me right as I wrapped my hand around the magazine. He stood only ten feet away. He saw the gun in my hand.

"You put that gun down," he said. "That's not how this works."

I yanked the magazine from my pocket and clicked it into the bottom of my gun. Walton said something about a level playing field to determine the victor. He then said something about being an apex predator. I glanced up to see him coming at me.

I racked the slide as Walton lunged at me, leaving his feet. I fired three times from holding my gun at my chest—I never had time to bring it up and aim. His body slammed into mine. My head cracked backward into the fender of the car. I felt the warmth of blood rolling over my face. It wasn't mine. I rolled my body to my right and pushed Walton's from me. I used the shoulder of my shirt to wipe his blood from my face and stared at him. He lay motionless, facedown. A pool of blood was forming beneath him. Blood was pumping from what had to have been a bullet hole on the left side of his neck.

I limped to the front of Steve's car and leaned against it. I kept aim on Walton's body. The sounds of sirens slowly began to build in the distance.

CHAPTER 40

A solid week had passed since I'd brought an end to Walton and his frenzy of taking lives. The impact from the car hitting my right foot broke a couple of bones, including a metatarsal. I forgot what the doctor said the other one was. What I knew was that there wasn't a ton that they could do. There would be no cast. I could only stay off it when possible, managing the pain and wearing a walking boot when I was out and about. I quickly came to despise the stupid boot that I was instructed to wear. The doc said I'd be in the thing for the better part of two months. It made me walk like Frankenstein and drew stares from everyone I limped past. I wore it as little as possible, opting for crutches instead. Aside from the foot, and who knew how many stitches between my head and arm, I wasn't too much worse for wear. The same couldn't be said about Walton. The three shots I fired had hit his neck, face, and forehead. Skip had said he was dead before he hit the ground.

I slowed in front of Steve's big yellow two-story house on the corner lot. The place was a couple of years old and had a hell of a pool area in the back. As nice as it was, it was still too master plan community for me. One three-thousand-square-foot house sat within feet of another of the same size. I enjoyed my neighbors but not that much. Plus, I wouldn't deal too well with a homeowners' association telling me what I could and couldn't do with my own damn property. Sasha stood in the front yard, probably waiting for us—she'd just buzzed us through the gates.

I gave her a wave and pulled up lengthwise across the base of Steve's driveway. I would be there only a couple of minutes, and his neighborhood didn't allow much in the way of street parking. I opened the driver's door.

"Hold on," Amy said. She hopped out, grabbed my crutches from the back, and rounded the front of the truck. Lucky, who'd been in the back, must have jumped out of Amy's side. She beat Amy to me. I leaned over and gave her a pet. Lucky had eyes on Sasha, who was walking down her driveway to greet us. "Go on. Go get her," I said. Lucky bolted toward Sasha.

Amy handed me my crutches and walked with me to Sasha, who was crouched and petting the dog.

Sasha looked up at me, moved her dark hair from her face with her finger, and stood. "How's the foot?"

"Still attached, I guess. Where's Grumpy?"

Steve hadn't been in the best of spirits since the injury. I didn't know if it was due to pain, being laid up, or his car being destroyed—maybe it was a combination of the three.

"Inside in his recliner in the living room and not in bed where he's supposed to be," Sasha said. "Go on in. He's watching some awful seventies cop movie."

"You got the pup?" I asked, looking at Amy.

Lucky was at the base of the single palm tree in Steve's yard, with eyes on a treed squirrel.

"She's fine. I don't think she's going anywhere," Amy said.

I crutched my way to the front door and walked in. Steve was on the recliner in his living room as Sasha had said. He faced the ceiling, snoring with his mouth hanging open. The television remote hung from his hand. His left leg from hip to ankle was encased in a big removable cast. One bullet had broken his femur, and another had gone through the meat of his upper thigh. They couldn't wrap him in a regular cast due to having to deal with the wounds. A pair of crutches leaned against the wall next to his chair.

"Fire!" I shouted.

Steve jerked awake and snapped his head toward me. It took him only a second. "Dick," he said.

I hobbled my way over to the big L-shaped couch and sat down. I rested my crutches beside me.

"Where's your Frankenboot?"

"At home," I said. "I'll be fine just like this."

Steve grumbled and rearranged himself in his chair. "Fine until you heal up and realize you can't walk right because one of your bones didn't set properly. You need to trust the doctor's advice and give it the needed time to heal."

It seemed that after spending two days in the hospital, he'd gotten himself a medical degree. "I'll be just fine," I said. "How are you feeling?"

"Me, I'm great," he said. "This leg is another story. It's

pissing me off. Make a mental note to not get shot."

"Noted," I said. "So, what did the doc tell you this morning?" Steve had had an appointment that morning, which, combined with our having to pass his house on our way to the lake, was the reason for the visit.

"Not a ton," he said. "Healing looks good. Too soon to give me any information as far as when I can get back to work, or even when I can get this stupid thing off and walk normal. Which can't come soon enough. I'm going to burn this plastic cast the second it comes off."

I figured I'd feed his line back to him. "You need to trust the doctor's advice and give it the needed time to heal," I said.

Steve gave me a quick glance and the finger.

I laughed and sank back into the couch.

"What's going on with the case?" Steve asked. "I saw it all over the news and papers. The woman that owned the minivan seems to be a talker."

"Yeah, she is," I said. "Think about it, though. A soccer mom who was carjacked by a wanted murderer, stuffed into a trunk, and left in an airport parking lot. That's a story she's going to tell for the rest of her life."

"True," Steve said. "What else?"

"There really isn't much that you don't know. Bank records show the rental cars, and his phone records put him near each crime at the time it occurred. The hair found in the Land Rover was a match to Kylie Bowe. We're still looking to see what was all below the surface—who he was, what his history was. Something to learn more about the guy and what the hell his motivations were. The cap wants the cold case guys to work it, so we'll see what they come up with. Maybe more killings can be attributed to him. Wade got a couple more things from Walton's laptop we recovered. The big thing was a photo of Walton posing with a deceased male. Someone indigenous to the jungle, the best we can tell. You can see a removed hand in the photo. We have to think that is the additional one we had in the house. A DNA test will reveal more, Colt said."

"Any idea when it was from? The photo."

"The data from the photo puts it a little over a year ago. No location, but the setting looks damn close if not identical to the photo he had in his house, posing with the darted man."

"Who took the photo?" Steve asked.

"Exactly. That was the first thing that I said. We tried to match up the date on the photo with something from his travel records. There was nothing."

"Damn," Steve said.

"It's going to be a work in progress. We'll see what else we can get from what we have. Maybe we can connect some more dots."

"Yeah, hopefully," Steve said. "You want a beer or something?"

"Nah, I'm driving," I said.

"All right. I'll have one, I guess," he said. He pointed toward the kitchen. "You're hurt less."

I shook my head, got up from the couch, and snatched my crutches. I hobbled my way to his refrigerator and grabbed him his beer. I noticed he had a photo of his Grand National stuck to the refrigerator door. I'd either never noticed it before or it was new since the car's demise. I got to the living room, handed Steve his beer, and plopped down.

"What did the insurance company tell you about the GN?"

"Total loss," he said. He cracked his beer and took a pull.

"Damn. Sorry," I said.

"I wouldn't have wanted it fixed, anyway. It just wouldn't have been the same. She was insured for the full appraisal amount, so I should get a pretty good check. As soon as I can move around again, I'll probably do some car shopping."

"New or another classic?" I asked.

"Probably something new. Maybe a new Camaro or Corvette or something. We'll see."

"Not another Grand National, though, huh?"

"Nah. Too many memories with the old one. It would be like I was cheating on her. Time to switch it up. Speaking of which, what are you going to do now that the Bronco is gone?"

"What do you mean?" I asked.

"For a car. Are you going to get another truck or what? Amy is going to get sick of carting you around really quick, and you can't just drive something from work all the time."

"The Bronco's fine," I said.

"It got shot all to hell," Steve said.

"I got it into my garage and swapped a radiator out and fixed a couple other little things that got dinged by bullets. I had a windshield overnighted to me from a Bronco restoration place, and Amy helped me put it in the other day. Aside from a few extra holes for ventilation, she's fine. Sitting outside right now with the boat strapped up to the back. We're heading up to Okeechobee to do a little fishing."

"You're serious," Steve said. He looked almost shocked. It was either shock or maybe disappointment.

"About fishing? Yeah, we're going to stay the night up there and hit the water first thing in the morning."

"No. About the truck," Steve said.

"Yeah. Like I said, a couple extra holes but all good. I'll probably weld some of them up, maybe leave some for style points."

"That thing is like a cockroach," he said.

I shrugged. "You guys wanna come?"

"Yes. Sasha would never go for it, though."

"Does she have to work tomorrow?" I asked.

"Off, but still."

"If you actually want to go, or feel up to it, we'll make it happen. I bet Amy can talk Sasha into it within ten minutes."

"What the hell am I going to do with this?" Steve pointed at his leg.

"It doesn't look like you have that much of a problem sitting on your ass. I bet you could do it just as well in a boat with a fishing rod in your hand."

Steve's face said he was contemplating.

"That's a yes," I said.

"I'm telling you, Sasha will shoot it down," Steve said.

"Ten bucks?" I asked. "Or twenty?"

"Twenty she says no."

"Forty says ten minutes and we'll be loading your gear up," I said.

"Deal," Steve said.

"Amy!" I called. I looked at Steve. "You better go start getting ready."

"Won't happen," he said.

We were on the road within a half hour. I had forty dollars in my front pocket and Steve and Sasha following us in my rearview mirror.

The End

For more books by E.H. Reinhard, please visit:
http://ehreinhard.com/

Made in the USA
Monee, IL
12 June 2024